MURDER AT ASHCOMBE HALL

A 1920'S HISTORICAL COSY MYSTERY

THE LADY ASHCOMBE MURDER MYSTERIES
BOOK ONE

FELICITY PENN

PUREREAD.COM

CONTENTS

DEAR READER, WELCOME TO ASHCOMBE...

READY TO SOLVE THE MYSTERY?

A lady, a legacy, and a deadly welcome...

When the new mistress of Ashcombe Hall raises her glass in celebration, she doesn't realise she's also toasting a murder.

Get ready for a charming 1920s historical mystery full of wit, danger, and quaint English village flair.

Turn the page—and step into Ashcombe Hall...

~

THE VICAR'S DAUGTHER

The motor juddered to a halt before Ashcombe Hall, and Cecily Grace Ashcombe—though she still thought of herself as simply the vicar's daughter—stared up at the imposing façade through rain-spotted spectacles. The estate loomed before her like something from a Gothic novel, all weathered Cotswold stone and diamond-paned windows that seemed to watch her with ancient, knowing eyes. Ivy clung to the walls with the tenacity of village gossips, and somewhere in the distance, a peacock shrieked as if announcing her arrival to the Oxfordshire countryside at large.

The October wind carried the scent of woodsmoke and dying leaves, a melancholy perfume that reminded her achingly of Father's last autumn sermon about seasons of change. Three weeks had passed since she'd buried both parents within a fortnight of each other—influenza taking them as swiftly and ruthlessly as it had claimed so many others this dreadful year of 1923. The familiar ache settled in her chest like a stone.

The curves of Oxfordshire lanes had stirred memories she'd thought safely buried beneath years of London anonymity and wartime urgency. Each hedgerow seemed to whisper recognition as the De Dion puttered through countryside that had shaped her earliest understanding of the world. Here was the ancient oak where she'd climbed as a girl, reading adventure stories whilst Father called for her to practice piano scales. There, the stone bridge where she'd dangled fishing lines with village children who'd since married, emigrated, or fallen in France.

The very air tasted different from London's coal-tinged breath—cleaner, sharper, carrying scents of her childhood that made her hands tremble slightly on the steering wheel. Wild roses still climbed the cottage walls, though the faces peering from doorways belonged to strangers or showed the lined evidence of decades she'd missed. The war years in France had taught her to compartmentalise emotion, to function despite exhaustion and horror, yet this gentle homecoming threatened her composure more thoroughly than artillery barrages ever had.

She'd left Little Codding as the eager young vicar's daughter, bound for London with dreams of independence and nursing training. Now she returned as something unrecognisable—a woman who'd held dying soldiers in her arms, who'd learned to function on two hours' sleep, who'd inherited responsibilities she'd never imagined. The girl who'd once known every sheep in every field had become a stranger to her own landscape, though it remained achingly, impossibly familiar.

"Right then, Pip," she murmured to the Jack Russell terrier bouncing enthusiastically on the leather seat beside her, his energy a stark contrast to the weight of grief she carried. "I suppose we'd better see what the good Lord has in store for us now."

Pip responded by promptly knocking her black mourning hat askew with his tail, a move that would have horrified her dear mother. Margaret Ashcombe had possessed very firm opinions about the proper maintenance of mourning attire, particularly when calling upon members of the peerage.

"Weeping may endure for a night," Cecily whispered, repeating one of Father's favourite verses, "but joy cometh in the morning." Though she couldn't quite imagine what form that joy might take in her current circumstances.

The front door of Ashcombe Hall opened with the sort of theatrical timing that suggested someone had been watching from behind the lace curtains. A woman emerged who could only be Mrs. Fotheringill, the housekeeper whose letter had summoned Cecily here with urgent but mysterious language about "His Lordship's final wishes" and "matters of considerable importance."

Mrs. Fotheringill was built rather like a well-fortified medieval castle—broad, imposing, and clearly designed to repel unwelcome visitors. Her grey hair was pulled back so severely it might have been used to tune a violin, and her black dress was starched to a degree that suggested she viewed wrinkles as a personal affront to the natural order. Her expression, as she took in Cecily's modest travelling dress and practical boots, conveyed the sort of polite disapproval usually reserved for slightly disappointing puddings.

"Miss Ashcombe," she announced, her voice carrying the authority of someone accustomed to maintaining order amongst wayward housemaids and visiting dignitaries alike. "His Lordship has been expecting you. Though I should mention he's been rather... particular about visitors of late."

Cecily gathered her courage along with her handbag and stepped from the motor car, grateful for the solid ground beneath her feet. The De Dion had served faithfully since Father's modest inheritance had allowed its purchase, but it possessed certain mechanical temperaments that required periodic roadside negotiations. Pip bounded out behind her with the enthusiasm of a small, furry cannonball, immediately beginning an intensive investigation of the gravelled drive.

"Thank you for your message, Mrs. Fotheringill. I do hope the Earl isn't too unwell? Your letter suggested some urgency..."

The housekeeper's eyes narrowed slightly as she took in Cecily's appearance—the faint smudge of motor oil on her glove where she'd adjusted the engine outside Chipping Norton, the small tear in her hem from helping an elderly gentleman with his punctured bicycle tyre, the decidedly unfashionable spectacles that proclaimed her more concerned with practicality than style.

"His Lordship specifically requested that you bring... that," Mrs. Fotheringill said, eyeing Pip with the expression one might reserve for a small but particularly suspect explosive device.

"Pip's actually quite well-behaved," Cecily lied with the cheerful optimism of someone whose faith extended to believing the best of both divine providence and incorrigible terriers.

As if summoned by this character reference, Pip chose that precise moment to discover a magnificent suit of armour standing sentinel in the entrance hall. With a delighted bark that echoed through the vaulted ceiling like a herald's trumpet, he launched himself at the medieval knight with the sort of enthusiasm usually reserved for Christmas morning.

The resulting crash would have done credit to a railway accident. When the dust and various pieces of priceless antiquity settled, Pip emerged from beneath a dented helmet with his tail wagging triumphantly, apparently under the impression that he'd successfully defeated a particularly well-dressed intruder.

"Quite," said Mrs. Fotheringill, her tone suggesting that she was already composing a strongly worded letter to someone about the declining standards of modern visitors and their insufficiently supervised pets.

Cecily's cheeks blazed crimson as she hurried to extract Pip from the wreckage of what had probably stood guard over the entrance for several centuries. "I'm terribly sorry! I'll certainly pay for any damages—"

"Miss Ashcombe." The voice came from the doorway to what appeared to be a library, warm and cultured despite its obvious weakness. Cecily looked up to see a tall, elegant gentleman with silver hair and eyes that held both kindness and an unmistakable weariness. Despite his burgundy dressing gown and the walking stick he leaned heavily upon, there was no mistaking the Earl of Harlecombe—Father's old friend from their Harrow days, though a friendship that had endured despite their vastly different chosen paths.

"Your Lordship." Cecily attempted what she hoped was an appropriate curtsey whilst still clutching Pip, who had apparently decided the Earl looked like excellent climbing material and was eyeing the silk cord of his dressing gown with professional interest.

"None of that nonsense between old friends, my dear girl." The Earl's voice carried the sort of cultivated accent that spoke of generations of privilege, yet underneath lay a warmth that reminded her powerfully of Father's own gentle authority. "Come, we've a great deal to discuss, and I rather fear time isn't precisely on our side."

As they made their way towards the library, Cecily couldn't help but marvel at the opulence surrounding her. This was a world far removed from the comfortable but modest vicarage of her childhood. Persian rugs that probably cost more than Father's annual stipend stretched across floors polished to mirror brightness, and oil paintings of stern-faced ancestors gazed down from every available wall space with the sort of expressions that suggested they found modern society distinctly wanting.

Crystal chandeliers cast rainbow patterns across cream-coloured walls, whilst mahogany furniture gleamed with the sort of loving care that spoke of generations of devoted servants. The very air seemed different here— scented with beeswax and lavender, old books and the faintest trace of expensive tobacco. It was elegant, intimidating, and utterly foreign to someone raised on simple furnishings and practical Christianity.

"Be strong and of good courage," Father's voice whispered in her memory, as clearly as if he stood beside her in his worn black cassock. "Fear not, nor be dismayed: for the Lord thy God is with thee whithersoever thou goest."

Drawing strength, Cecily squared her shoulders. After all, she'd nursed wounded soldiers through the worst fighting of the war, had held dying boys' hands whilst shells exploded overhead and organised field hospitals under conditions that would have tested seasoned military officers. Surely she could manage a civilised conversation with an elderly earl, even if his library did contain more leather-bound volumes than the cathedral library at Worcester.

The Earl settled himself carefully into a wing-backed chair positioned beside a cheerful fire, the flames casting warm light across features that spoke of both breeding and character. He gestured for Cecily to take the seat opposite—a beautiful piece upholstered in sage green silk that probably cost more than most people earned in a year.

Pip immediately began an intensive investigation of a Persian rug, his nose twitching at scents that were clearly far more fascinating than the polite conversation his mistress seemed intent on having. The rug, Cecily noted with growing alarm, appeared to be both priceless and extremely delicate.

"You're wondering why I've summoned you here," the Earl said, his eyes twinkling with familiar warmth despite the obvious pain that shadowed his pale features. "Particularly when you've only just laid your dear parents to rest."

Cecily nodded, not quite trusting her voice. The grief was still too raw, too immediate. Father's gentle wisdom and Mother's practical love had been the foundation stones of her world. Without them, she felt rather like a ship cut loose from its moorings in distinctly choppy waters.

"They were taken too soon," she managed finally. "Though Father always said the Lord's timing is perfect, even when we cannot understand it."

"Your father was the finest man I ever had the privilege to know," the Earl said softly, his voice carrying decades of respect and affection. "Did you know we were at school together? Harrow, though I suspect Thomas never mentioned it. He wasn't one for dwelling on old associations, particularly those that smacked of privilege he'd deliberately chosen to set aside."

"He spoke of you often, sir," Cecily replied, remembering Father's fond references to "young Harlecombe" and his occasional worry over his old friend's increasing isolation. "He said you were the only member of the aristocracy worth knowing, though I suspect that was rather uncharitable of him towards your peers."

The Earl's laugh was warm but breathless. "Probably quite accurate, I'm afraid. The peerage hasn't exactly covered itself in glory in recent years—too much privilege, insufficient purpose, and an alarming tendency to mistake tradition for wisdom." His expression grew serious, and Cecily noticed how his hand trembled slightly as he reached for a glass of water on the side table. "Which brings me rather directly to why you're here, my dear."

Before he could continue further, a tremendous crash echoed from somewhere in the depths of the house, followed by what sounded distinctly like a cat's declaration of war. Pip's ears shot up with the enthusiasm of a cavalry officer hearing the trumpet charge, his entire body vibrating with barely contained excitement.

"Ah," said the Earl, apparently entirely unsurprised by the domestic catastrophe. "That would be Duchess—my late wife's Persian cat. She has rather strong opinions about most things, but particularly about uninvited guests in her domain."

As if summoned by the mention of her name, a magnificent silver Persian appeared in the library doorway like a small, furry empress making a grand entrance. She took one disdainful look at Pip, who was practically bouncing with the desire to make her acquaintance, and issued what could only be described as a formal challenge to single combat.

Pip, never one to ignore such a clear invitation to adventure, responded with equal enthusiasm and considerably less dignity.

What followed could only be described as the most aristocratic chase sequence ever to grace the hallowed halls of an English country estate. Duchess swept through the library with the fluid grace of a queen in temporary exile, leaping from Persian rug to Chippendale chair to marble mantelpiece with the sort of effortless elegance that spoke of generations of careful breeding. Pip pursued with the determination of a small, enthusiastic hurricane, scattering silk cushions and causing a minor avalanche of leather-bound first editions to tumble from their carefully arranged shelves.

"Pip, no!" Cecily called, half-rising from her chair in mortification as her dog demonstrated why he'd been banned from three separate Sunday services. But the Earl raised a gentle hand, his eyes bright with amusement.

"Let them sort it out between themselves," he said, chuckling despite his obvious fatigue. "Duchess has ruled this house with an iron paw for eight years, but she appreciates genuine spirit when she encounters it. Your Pip reminds me rather of myself at his age—all enthusiasm and questionable judgement."

Indeed, as if to prove his point, the chase concluded with both combatants somehow wedged behind a particularly enormous atlas of the British Empire, from which location emanated a series of cautiously respectful sniffs and the beginning of what might charitably be called a negotiated cease-fire.

"Now then, come sit," the Earl said, settling back in his chair as Cecily retrieved a slightly dusty but thoroughly pleased Pip. "As I was attempting to explain, you're here because I have something rather important to discuss with you."

2

THE EARL'S FINAL WISH

Cecily resumed her seat, Pip curling in her lap with the satisfied air of a diplomat who'd successfully concluded delicate international negotiations. Despite his misbehaviour, having his warm weight against her provided a comfort she desperately needed in these overwhelming surroundings.

"I confess myself quite curious, your Lordship. Your letter was rather mysterious, and Mrs. Fotheringill seemed... well, concerned."

The Earl's expression grew solemn, and she noticed how the lines of pain around his eyes deepened. "My dear child, I'm dying. No, please don't look like that—I've made my peace with it months ago. The doctors give me perhaps a week, possibly less. My heart, you see, has decided it's had quite enough of keeping me alive, and I can hardly blame it after seventy-three years of faithful service."

Cecily felt her breath catch, the casual way he spoke of death reminding her painfully of her recent losses. "Surely there's something Dr. Bell can do—"

"Freddie's been magnificent, actually. Keeps me comfortable, doesn't lecture me about slowing down, and brings excellent whisky when she thinks I need cheering up. But we both know there's nothing more to be done medically." The Earl leaned forward slightly, his voice growing stronger with purpose. "What concerns me isn't my own departure—that's in God's hands now. What keeps me awake at night is the question of Ashcombe Hall and everything that goes with it."

"Surely you have family," Cecily said carefully. "Cousins, perhaps distant relatives who—"

"Oh, I have family indeed." The Earl's tone carried a distinct chill. "Lord Oswald Crowthorne, my late wife's nephew, has been circling this estate like a particularly unpleasant vulture for the better part of a year. He's my heir presumptive, legally speaking, though I'd rather bequeath everything to Duchess than see him get his grasping hands on this place."

"I'm certain he cannot be as dreadful as all that," Cecily said diplomatically, though something in the Earl's expression suggested otherwise.

"Oh, but he can, my dear girl. He absolutely can." The Earl's voice hardened with distaste. "Oswald would sell off the tenant farms to the highest bidder, dismiss half the household staff to cut expenses, and probably convert the Hall into some ghastly commercial hotel for wealthy Americans wanting to experience 'authentic English aristocracy.' He views everything in terms of immediate profit rather than long-term stewardship."

Cecily frowned. "But surely there's something in the entailment that would prevent—"

"Ah, but here's where providence smiles upon us." The Earl's eyes brightened considerably. "Ashcombe isn't actually entailed, you see. My great-grandfather was either remarkably progressive for his time or simply bloody-minded enough to spite his relatives—family history remains divided on the question. The 1870 resettlement deed broke the entail, leaving the house outright to the Earl. The estate can pass to whomever I choose, regardless of bloodline or traditional inheritance law."

He paused, fixing her with a direct gaze that seemed to see straight through to her soul.

"And I choose you, Cecily."

The fire crackled in the sudden silence. Somewhere in the distance, a clock chimed the half-hour. Pip, sensing the gravity of the moment, actually ceased his investigation of interesting carpet smells and sat perfectly still.

"I... I beg your pardon?" Cecily whispered.

"I want you to inherit Ashcombe Hall," the Earl said, his voice growing stronger with conviction. "All of it—the estate, the farms, the investments, the responsibility for our tenants and staff, and yes, the very considerable wealth that accompanies such a position. I've watched you over the years, my dear, seen how you cared for your father's parish even as a young girl, how you boldly ventured to London, and served our wounded soldiers with such courage and compassion. Thomas spoke constantly of your wisdom, your integrity, your remarkable ability to see past society's surface conventions to the true heart of matters."

Cecily stared at him as if he'd suddenly announced his intention to take up competitive balloon dancing. "But I'm nobody special! A country vicar's daughter with ink stains on her fingers and motor oil under her nails. I wouldn't even know which fork to use at a proper formal dinner!"

"My dear girl," the Earl said gently, "I've attended more formal dinners than any civilised person should have to endure, and I can assure you that knowing which fork to use is monumentally overrated compared to having the courage to do what's right, the wisdom to care properly for those placed in your charge, and the heart to understand that great wealth is primarily a responsibility rather than merely a privilege."

The magnitude of what he was proposing began to settle over her like a heavy cloak. "But the staff, the tenants, people who've known proper aristocracy for generations —they'd never accept someone like me."

"They'll accept you because you'll earn their respect through your actions," the Earl said firmly. "Just as your father earned the love of his parishioners not through grand gestures but through daily kindness and unwavering integrity. Besides," he added with a slight smile, "Mrs. Fotheringill has been running this place quite efficiently for twenty years. She'll teach you everything you need to know about household management, provided you approach her with appropriate respect for her expertise."

Before Cecily could formulate a coherent response to this extraordinary proposition, the library door burst open with the sort of dramatic timing that suggested professional eavesdropping had been employed. Mrs. Fotheringill swept in, her expression tight with barely controlled emotion and righteous indignation.

"Your Lordship," she announced, her voice vibrating with suppressed feelings, "I couldn't help but overhear certain portions of your conversation—"

"How remarkable," the Earl observed mildly. "I could have sworn that door was closed. Perhaps the hinges need oiling?"

Mrs. Fotheringill's colour rose slightly, but her composure remained admirably intact. "I feel compelled to express certain concerns, your Lordship. Miss Ashcombe is undoubtedly a perfectly pleasant young lady, but to consider leaving the estate to someone with no experience in managing a great house, no understanding of proper social protocols, no knowledge of estate management—"

"Mrs. Fotheringill," Cecily interrupted gently, recognising the genuine distress beneath the housekeeper's formal objections, "I completely understand your reservations. I'd have precisely the same concerns if I were in your position."

The housekeeper turned to her with something approaching surprise. "You would?"

"Absolutely. You've devoted decades of your life to maintaining this house's standards, preserving its traditions, training staff to uphold its reputation. The thought of someone like me simply walking in and potentially undoing all your careful work must be rather like watching someone hand a priceless violin to an enthusiastic but untrained child."

Mrs. Fotheringill's rigid posture softened fractionally. "That's... that's actually a remarkably apt comparison."

"Then perhaps," Cecily continued, drawing on her experience managing difficult hospital administrators during the war, "you might consider helping me learn? I certainly cannot imagine attempting to oversee a place like this without the guidance of someone who truly understands its complexities."

The Earl watched this exchange with obvious delight, though Cecily noticed his breathing seemed to be growing more laboured. "You see, Mrs. Fotheringill? I told you she possessed both wisdom and humility."

The housekeeper looked between them, clearly wrestling with conflicting emotions. Finally, she cleared her throat with the air of someone making a momentous decision. "I suppose... that is to say, if Miss Ashcombe were genuinely willing to learn proper procedures and maintain appropriate standards..."

"I should be honoured by your instruction," Cecily said with complete sincerity.

Mrs. Fotheringill nodded curtly, though something in her expression suggested cautious approval. "Very well then. Though I do hope you'll address that dog's behaviour. There are certain standards that must be maintained in a house of this quality."

As if deliberately proving her point, Pip chose that precise moment to emerge from beneath a chair with what appeared to be an extremely valuable leather bookmark dangling from his mouth like a small, literary trophy.

"Pip!" Cecily scolded, but the Earl was laughing—or attempting to, though the sound carried a worrying wheeze that made her nursing instincts immediately alert.

"I think..." he began breathlessly, his hand moving to his chest, "I think perhaps I should rest now. The excitement has been rather... rather overwhelming."

Cecily was at his side immediately, her wartime medical training taking complete control. His colour had shifted to an alarming grey, his breathing rapid and shallow despite his attempts to remain composed. She checked his pulse with practiced efficiency whilst mentally cataloguing symptoms that spoke of serious cardiac distress.

"Mrs. Fotheringill, please send for Dr. Bell immediately," she said with calm authority. "Tell her it's urgent."

The housekeeper hurried from the room with uncharacteristic speed, and Cecily helped the Earl settle more comfortably in his chair, loosening his collar and ensuring his airway remained clear. Pip, sensing the gravity of the situation with the remarkable intuition of animals, abandoned his literary conquest and settled himself quietly at the Earl's feet.

"Don't look so terribly worried, my dear," the Earl whispered, his eyes still kind despite the obvious pain. "I've had a good run of it, and I'm not afraid of what comes next. 'In my Father's house are many mansions,' after all. Your father and I discussed that passage many times over the years."

Cecily felt her throat tighten with emotion. "Please don't

speak as though you're giving up. Dr. Bell will be here shortly—"

"Cecily." The Earl's voice carried surprising firmness despite its weakness. "Before anything else happens, I need your word. Promise me you'll accept this responsibility. Promise you'll take care of this place and these people who depend on it. They need someone who understands that privilege exists to serve others, not merely to indulge oneself."

She looked into his eyes, saw the absolute faith reflected there, and felt something profound shift within her heart. Perhaps it was divine providence, perhaps simple human compassion, but she found herself nodding with growing certainty.

"I promise, your Lordship. I'll do everything in my power to prove worthy of your trust."

The Earl smiled with such peaceful satisfaction that it transformed his pain-lined features entirely. "Good. Cartwright is waiting outside with the papers already prepared—everything proper and binding, though I suspect Oswald will have considerable opinions about the arrangement." He managed a weak chuckle. "I do hope you won't allow him to intimidate you."

"I've dealt with army colonels, field marshals, and Her Majesty Queen Alexandra herself during hospital inspections," Cecily said with more confidence than she entirely felt. "I believe I can manage one disgruntled relative."

"That's my brave girl," the Earl murmured, his eyes beginning to drift closed. "Your father would be extraordinarily proud of the woman you've become."

A discreet rap sounded on the door.

Mr St John opened it a crack. "Mr Lionel Cartwright to see you, my lord."

"Show him in," the Earl said.

Solicitor Cartwright adjusted his spectacles.

"The late Earl anticipated any challenge, Miss Ashcombe. By letters patent dated 15 November 1922, His Majesty created the Barony of Ashcombe, with remainder to you and your heirs. You are therefore Baroness—Lady—Ashcombe in your own right."

Cecily's breath caught. The words seemed to hang in the fire-lit air, too momentous to grasp. The Earl smiled weakly, wholly satisfied. "Quite official, you see."

3

WHEN THE BELL TOLLS

Dr. Winifred Bell arrived precisely eighteen minutes later, striding into the library with the sort of brisk, no-nonsense efficiency that had made her one of the most respected battlefield surgeons of the entire war. During 1915-18 she served with the Scottish Women's Hospitals at Royaumont, one of the few units that took female surgeons right to the Western Front, and the experience still shaped her unflappable manner. She remained impressively tall, sharp-eyed, and possessed of the ability to assess any medical situation with a single comprehensive glance.

"Freddie," Cecily said, relief flooding through her at the sight of her former colleague and friend.

"Well, well. Cecily Ashcombe, as I live and breathe." Dr. Bell's examination of the Earl was swift, thorough, and unfortunately conclusive. Her expression grew increasingly grave as she checked his failing pulse and listened to his struggling heart. "How long has he been in this condition?"

"He seemed reasonably well initially, but grew excited during our conversation, then his breathing became laboured..."

Dr. Bell nodded, her hands infinitely gentle as she made the Earl as comfortable as possible. "His heart's been failing progressively for months. I've been treating him as effectively as medical science allows, but..." She shook her head sombrely. "There's nothing more that can be done, I'm afraid. It's simply a matter of time now."

The Earl passed away peacefully just as the grandfather clock in the entrance hall chimed nine o'clock. Dr. Bell closed his eyes with the reverent care that Cecily remembered from countless field hospitals, and they stood together in respectful silence, paying tribute to a man who had lived with dignity and faced death with grace.

"Well," Dr. Bell said finally, her voice professionally gentle but warm with genuine affection, "I believe congratulations are in order, Lady Ashcombe."

Cecily started at the unfamiliar title. "I beg your pardon?"

"Mrs. Fotheringill provided me with certain details whilst I was preparing my medical bag. Quite the inheritance, from what I understand. Though I can't say I'm entirely surprised—His Lordship spoke very highly of you whenever we discussed the estate's future."

"I still cannot quite believe any of this is real," Cecily admitted, sinking into her chair as the full magnitude of what had transpired began to settle upon her shoulders like an enormous, invisible mantle. "This morning I was simply Cecily who used to live in the vicarage, worried about paying the coal bill and wondering whether to keep Father's old motor. Now I'm apparently responsible for an entire estate, a household full of servants, tenant farmers, and..." She gestured helplessly at the opulent surroundings.

"And one extremely incorrigible terrier who seems to have developed expensive literary tastes," Dr. Bell added dryly, observing Pip's latest bibliographical discovery amongst the scattered books.

Cecily rescued what appeared to be a first edition of Paradise Lost from certain canine critique and gathered Pip into her arms. "What on earth am I to do, Freddie? I haven't the faintest idea how to be a lady of the manor."

"My dear girl," Dr. Bell said, settling into the Earl's chair with the sort of casual disregard for social protocol that Cecily rather envied, "if four years of war taught me anything worthwhile, it's that half of any important battle consists simply of showing up and doing whatever needs doing next. You managed to maintain an entire hospital ward full of wounded soldiers during the worst fighting of the Somme, keeping them alive and reasonably cheerful whilst shells exploded overhead and supplies ran desperately short. I rather suspect you can manage one English country estate and its associated complications."

"Even when it comes complete with disapproving household staff and mysterious family members who are bound to be rather upset about inheritance arrangements?"

"Especially then," Dr. Bell said firmly. "Though I would suggest preparing yourself for some particularly interesting social occasions. Oswald Crowthorne is not known for accepting disappointment with good grace—or indeed, accepting it at all."

As if summoned by the mention of difficult family dynamics, Mrs. Fotheringill reappeared in the library doorway, her expression carefully neutral but somehow conveying deep consideration of changed circumstances.

"Lady Ashcombe," she said, the unfamiliar title delivered with only the faintest suggestion of adjustment anxiety, "I've taken the liberty of preparing the Rose Room for your use tonight. I thought you might prefer somewhere comfortable whilst we... whilst we make necessary arrangements."

Cecily looked up at her, struck by the genuine kindness beneath the housekeeper's invariably formal manner. "Thank you, Mrs. Fotheringill. That's extremely thoughtful of you."

"And perhaps," the housekeeper continued with visible effort towards conciliation, "we might discuss household schedules and estate procedures tomorrow morning? I find that maintaining familiar routines helps considerably during times of... significant transition."

"I should like that very much indeed," Cecily said warmly. "I have an enormous amount to learn, and I'm grateful for your willingness to teach me."

Mrs. Fotheringill's expression softened almost imperceptibly, the first crack in her professional reserve. "Well then. I suppose we shall muddle through together, one way or another."

As Dr. Bell made discreet arrangements for the Earl's body and Mrs. Fotheringill bustled off to organise various mysterious domestic necessities involving clean linens and appropriate flowers, Cecily found herself alone in the library with Pip and the profound weight of a conversation that had changed everything.

The fire had burnt low, casting dancing shadows across the leather-bound volumes and oil paintings that were now, somehow, inexplicably hers. Rain had begun pattering against the diamond-paned windows, and somewhere in the house's depths, a clock chimed the quarter-hour with melodious precision.

"Trust in the Lord with all thine heart," she whispered, finding comfort in a cherished verse, "and lean not unto thine own understanding. In all thy ways acknowledge him, and he shall direct thy paths."

Pip, apparently sensing her need for reassurance, abandoned his scholarly investigations in favour of settling his warm, solid weight across her feet. It was a small gesture, but somehow it made the enormous responsibility she'd just inherited feel slightly more manageable—as though she needn't face it entirely alone.

Tomorrow would bring lawyers and legal papers, household accounts that needed understanding, tenant farmers requiring introduction, and the daunting prospect of learning to navigate a social world she'd only ever observed from the respectable distance of the parish clergy. There would undoubtedly be complications with family members, challenges from the local gentry, and probably a great deal of fuss from various quarters about the unprecedented nature of her inheritance.

But tonight, she was simply Cecily, sitting in a beautiful library with her faithful dog and the cherished memory of a good man's absolute trust in her character and capabilities.

Outside, the October wind picked up, sending autumn leaves dancing across the terrace like small golden butterflies. A night bird called somewhere in the darkness, its voice clear and wild and somehow hopeful.

Ashcombe Hall settled around her with the comfortable

creaks and sighs of a well-loved house welcoming its new mistress home.

"Well then, Pip," she said softly, scratching behind his ears as he dozed contentedly. "I suppose we'd better prove ourselves worthy of such faith."

And despite everything—the grief, the uncertainty, the overwhelming magnitude of what lay ahead—Cecily found herself smiling as she spoke the words.

After all, the Lord had never yet given her a burden too heavy to bear, and she rather suspected He wasn't about to start now.

4

LADY CECILY REBORN

The Rose Room lived up to its name in every particular, from the climbing roses painted across cream silk wallpaper to the actual rose garden visible through mullioned windows that caught the early morning light like scattered diamonds. Cecily woke slowly, her mind taking several precious moments to reconcile the Egyptian cotton sheets and four-poster bed with her memories of the modest vicarage bedroom she'd occupied for twenty-nine years.

Then reality settled upon her with the weight of a cathedral bell.

She was Lady Ashcombe now. The mistress of an estate that sprawled across more acres than she could properly comprehend, responsible for tenants and staff and traditions that stretched back generations. The enormity of it made her feel rather like a sparrow who'd been asked to captain a naval vessel.

Pip, suffering no such existential concerns about their dramatically altered circumstances, stirred beside her with a luxurious stretch that suggested he'd adapted to aristocratic living with remarkable ease. His investigation of the room's corners led to the discovery of a silk-upholstered chair that clearly required immediate attention from his talented teeth.

"Absolutely not," Cecily said firmly, extracting him from what was undoubtedly a priceless antique. "We're quite enough of a disruption without adding furniture destruction to our catalogue of social infractions."

A gentle knock interrupted this domestic negotiation. A young housemaid entered bearing a silver tea service that caught the morning light like something from a fairy tale. The girl—she couldn't be more than seventeen—executed a curtsey with practised grace whilst managing the tray with impressive skill.

"Good morning, my lady," she said, her soft Oxfordshire accent immediately comforting. "Mrs. Fotheringill thought you might appreciate some tea before breakfast. I'm Mary, my lady."

The casual formality of being addressed as 'my lady' sent an odd flutter through Cecily's chest—part pride, part terror, and a substantial measure of disbelief that any of this was real.

"Thank you, Mary. That's extremely thoughtful." Cecily accepted the delicate china teacup, noting absently that it probably cost more than most families spent on crockery in a decade. "Though I should mention that I expect to be in residence permanently. I will be making arrangements regarding my former accommodations, but this most unexpectedly will be home to me now."

Mary's eyes widened with genuine surprise. "Yes, my lady. Quite the change for everyone, if you don't mind me saying. Mrs. Fotheringill's been up since five, making certain everything's arranged properly for your first day."

After Mary departed, Cecily threw open the Rose Room's windows and breathed deeply of the crisp October air. The estate spread before her like an illuminated manuscript—manicured lawns giving way to parkland dotted with ancient oaks, formal gardens maintaining their geometric elegance even in autumn's grip, and beyond it all, the gentle Oxfordshire hills rolling towards horizons that seemed impossibly distant from the modest world of her upbringing.

Somewhere out there lay Little Codding, the village that had somehow become her responsibility along with everything else. The thought was simultaneously thrilling and utterly terrifying.

"Be strong and of good courage," she whispered, "The Lord thy God is with thee whithersoever thou goest."

Even if 'whithersoever' included navigating social waters for which twenty-nine years in a vicarage had provided absolutely no preparation.

The house itself seemed to understand its state of mourning, settling into a respectful quietude that muffled even the familiar sounds of morning preparation. Floorboards that might ordinarily creak with purposeful activity now whispered their protests. The very walls appeared to absorb conversation, as though the manor's stones themselves observed the proprieties of grief.

Everything within Ashcombe Hall's walls acknowledged that death had visited, and that proper respect must be maintained until enough time had passed for life to resume its normal volume.

Even Pip, for once, had awakened without his customary enthusiastic barking, as though some canine instinct recognised the need for decorum during this delicate period of transition.

The morning room proved to be a pleasant space decorated in shades of butter yellow and cream, with French doors opening onto a terrace where peacocks strutted about with supreme confidence in their ornamental importance. Mrs. Fotheringill had arranged a breakfast that could have fed Wellington's entire staff— silver serving dishes gleaming like small suns, eggs prepared in more variations than Cecily had known existed, and enough bacon to supply a small market town.

"Good heavens," Cecily murmured, surveying the bounty. "Mrs. Fotheringill, surely this is rather excessive for one person?"

The housekeeper, who had been arranging chrysanthemums with military precision, turned with carefully neutral expression. "I wasn't certain of your preferences, my lady. His late Lordship appreciated having options available."

Cecily helped herself to modest portions whilst Pip positioned himself strategically beneath the table, radiating hope and professional charm. "This is absolutely lovely, but please don't feel obligated to such elaborate preparations on my account. A vicar's daughter learns to appreciate simple fare."

Something shifted almost imperceptibly in Mrs. Fotheringill's posture—not precisely warming, but a recognition that her new mistress possessed no pretensions about her origins.

"As you wish, my lady. Though I should mention that the village has become considerably... animated regarding yesterday's developments."

"Animated in what fashion?" Cecily asked, though she rather suspected the answer wouldn't be entirely comfortable.

"Young Timothy from the post office arrived with correspondence in quite a state of excitement. News of your inheritance appears to have spread through Little Codding with remarkable efficiency. There's been extensive discussion at the pub."

Before Cecily could respond to this diplomatic phrasing, a commotion from the front drive announced an arrival that sounded like a small but enthusiastic cavalry charge. Pip immediately abandoned his breakfast surveillance in favour of investigating this promising development, his bark adding considerably to the general cacophony.

"That'll be Miss Elsie," Mrs. Fotheringill said with resignation. "I took the liberty of sending word yesterday evening."

Cecily's spirits lifted immediately. Elsie Pickering had been her dearest friend since childhood—the former vicarage housekeeper's daughter who'd grown up alongside her in a whirlwind of shared adventures and unshakeable loyalty that had survived even the vast social gap that now yawned between them.

The breakfast room door burst open with characteristic force, admitting a whirlwind of energy in a practical coat and hat jammed onto chestnut curls with more haste than precision. Elsie entered every room as though storming a particularly important fortress.

"Cecily Grace Ashcombe!" she announced. "You absolute dark horse! When I received Mrs. F's message, I thought someone was having me on. 'Lady Ashcombe' indeed—as if you weren't sufficient trouble when you were merely the vicar's daughter!"

"Elsie," Cecily said, rising to embrace her friend with profound relief. "Thank goodness you're here. I feel rather like someone who's wandered into the wrong life entirely."

Elsie returned the embrace enthusiastically before stepping back to survey the morning room's elegant appointments with frank assessment. She slapped a folded copy of *The Times* down beside the teapot.

"It even made the Court Circular: 'Letters patent creating the Barony of Ashcombe for Miss Cecily Rose Ashcombe were this day enrolled.' Quite the distinction."

Cecily continued to look rather like a deer caught in headlights at the thought of it.

"You've certainly landed on your feet," gushed Elsie proudly, "This is considerably grander than the vicarage breakfast nook."

"Rather," Cecily agreed dryly. "Mrs. Fotheringill, may I present Miss Elsie Pickering? Elsie, Mrs. Fotheringill manages this household with extraordinary skill."

The two women regarded each other with the careful evaluation of experienced professionals recognising a colleague. Mrs. Fotheringill's expression suggested cautious approval of Elsie's obvious competence, whilst

Elsie's quick glance around the room conveyed proper appreciation for the housekeeper's evident standards.

"Miss Pickering," Mrs. Fotheringill said formally. "Your mother spoke of you often during her time at the vicarage. She was very proud of your war service."

"Thank you. Mother always maintained that the Ashcombe household set the county's finest standards." Elsie's response carried exactly the right note of respect whilst establishing her own credentials. "I do hope I might assist during this transition. Cecily and I have been managing various domestic disasters together since childhood."

"I was rather hoping you might consider staying permanently," Cecily interjected. "That is, if you're willing to help me navigate the complexities of being a proper lady of the manor. I suspect I'll need every possible advantage."

Elsie's face lit with delight. "Try and stop me! Though I should warn you, Mrs. Fotheringill, that I possess very strong opinions about most subjects, particularly regarding Cecily's welfare."

"So I had gathered," Mrs. Fotheringill replied, though her tone suggested this wasn't necessarily criticism. "Perhaps we might discuss appropriate arrangements after breakfast? I believe Lady Ashcombe was planning to introduce herself properly to the village this morning."

"Excellent notion," Elsie said, settling beside Cecily and helping herself to tea with easy familiarity. "Little Codding is absolutely buzzing with speculation, from what I observed during my journey here. Mrs. Tuggles at the post office was practically vibrating with excitement."

"What manner of speculation?" Cecily asked, though she wasn't entirely certain she wished to know.

"The usual village theories. Half the population believes you must have bewitched poor His Lordship with mysterious feminine wiles, whilst the other half suspects scandalous family secrets. Canon Bott apparently fainted when he heard the news, though that might have been unrelated—he's appeared rather peaked lately."

Mrs. Fotheringill sniffed disapprovingly. "Village gossip rarely demonstrates charity or accuracy. Though I confess Canon Bott has seemed somewhat... excitable since assuming your dear father's position."

"Father always said replacing a beloved vicar was rather like following a particularly successful theatrical performance," Cecily observed. "The congregation is predisposed to find fault with any successor, regardless of their actual merits."

"Quite so. Though in Canon Bott's case, certain recreational activities have raised eyebrows amongst traditional parishioners."

Elsie leaned forward with keen interest. "Recreational activities?"

"He writes," Mrs. Fotheringill said in tones usually reserved for discussing contagious diseases. "Novels. Mystery novels featuring murders and suspicious circumstances, published under some ridiculous pseudonym."

"How wonderfully scandalous!" Elsie exclaimed. "A vicar who writes murder mysteries—whatever next?"

Cecily found herself rather charmed by the notion. "I think it sounds perfectly delightful. If one is to write fiction, one might as well create something entertaining."

Before Mrs. Fotheringill could elaborate on the inappropriateness of clergymen dabbling in sensational literature, another arrival announced itself with the steady throb of a well-maintained motor engine and someone whistling a melancholy tune.

"That will be Mr. Miles Penrose," Mrs. Fotheringill said, moving to the window. "His late Lordship's chauffeur. He wishes to discuss resuming his position."

"I should very much like to meet him," Cecily said. "Might he join us here? I find formal interviews rather intimidating."

Mrs. Fotheringill's expression conveyed polite horror at this breach of protocol. "My lady, it would be most irregular to conduct household business in the morning room."

"Mrs. Fotheringill," Cecily said gently but firmly, "I suspect my success in this role will require establishing approaches that suit my nature whilst respecting tradition. Perhaps we might compromise with the garden terrace?"

The housekeeper considered this diplomatic solution. "Very well, my lady. That would provide appropriate dignity whilst accommodating a more... informal atmosphere."

5

A FINAL FAREWELL

The day of the Earl's funeral dawned grey and solemn, as though the very heavens had arranged themselves in mourning dress for the Earl of Harlecombe's final journey. From her window in the Rose Room, Cecily watched as carriages began arriving at Ashcombe Hall in steady procession, their black-clad occupants emerging like crows gathering for some ancient ritual she barely understood.

She had inherited not only an estate and title, but the obligation to serve as chief mourner for a man she had met only a few times—a curious circumstance that had set tongues wagging from Little Codding to Oxford. The weight of propriety pressed upon her shoulders like a mantle of lead as Mrs. Fotheringill supervised the funeral preparations.

"The Bishop of Oxford himself will officiate," the housekeeper had announced that morning, her tone suggesting this episcopal presence represented both tremendous honour and considerable opportunity for disaster. "His Grace knew the Earl for forty years. They served together on the cathedral board."

Cecily adjusted her black dress, hastily procured from the village seamstress and still smelling faintly of lavender and anxiety, and descended to meet the mourners who had come to pay their respects to a man whose final act had been to transform her life entirely.

The small Ashcombe chapel, where the Earl himself had requested his funeral address take place, had been decorated with white lilies and autumn chrysanthemums, their heavy fragrance competing with the scent of beeswax candles and the particular mustiness that seemed endemic to ancient stone buildings. Every pew filled with faces she didn't recognise. Distant relations, fellow peers, local dignitaries, and representatives from the various charitable organisations the Earl had supported with quiet generosity.

Canon Bott, the new parish priest, looked rather like a nervous rabbit presiding over a gathering of foxes, as he managed the preliminary arrangements whilst casting anxious glances toward the Bishop's magnificent purple vestments. His hands trembled slightly as he consulted his prayer book, clearly overwhelmed by the prospect of serving at such an elevated ceremony under Episcopal supervision.

"Dearly beloved," the Bishop began, his voice carrying the authority of decades spent addressing congregations from cathedral pulpits, "we are gathered together in the sight of God to commit to His keeping the soul of our brother, Edward Algernon Fitzwilliam, sixth Earl of Harlecombe, and to celebrate a life dedicated to service, stewardship, and the quiet virtues that mark a true Christian gentleman."

Cecily found herself studying the congregation, wondering which of these solemn faces had known the Earl personally and which had come merely to observe the spectacle of a penniless vicar's daughter inheriting one of Oxfordshire's most prestigious estates. Several elderly ladies in the front pews dabbed at their eyes with black-edged handkerchiefs, whilst others maintained the sort of composed expression that suggested professional mourning experience.

The service proceeded with ancient dignity through familiar prayers and hymns that reminded her powerfully of Father and the countless funerals they had attended together in Little Codding's modest church. "I am the resurrection and the life," the Bishop intoned, and Cecily felt the comforting certainty of words that transcended social anxiety and temporal concerns about inheritance propriety.

The irony was not lost on her—within a year, she had mourned the deaths of the two people who had shaped her entire world and inherited responsibility for a man whose friendship with her father had remained largely mysterious until its extraordinary culmination.

The Harlecombe family vault, cut into the hillside near the church, represented centuries of careful stewardship and accumulated tradition. Names carved in marble stretched back to the Norman Conquest, chronicling generations of Earls who had managed these lands through wars, plagues, political upheavals, and social transformations that had swept away lesser houses.

As the Bishop spoke the final committal prayers, Cecily found herself making a silent promise to the man whose generosity had so dramatically altered her circumstances. Whatever his reasons for choosing her as his successor—friendship with Father, faith in her character, or simply the absence of more conventional heirs—she would prove worthy of his trust.

"Earth to earth, ashes to ashes, dust to dust," the Bishop concluded, and the Earl of Harlecombe was laid to rest among his ancestors whilst the October wind scattered golden leaves across the ancient stones like nature's own tribute to the passing of time.

The reception at Ashcombe Hall afterwards proved a more daunting prospect than the funeral itself. Mrs. Fotheringill had prepared refreshments suitable for a hundred guests, and the drawing rooms filled with the particular blend of grief, curiosity, and social calculation that marked such gatherings. Cecily moved among the mourners with what she hoped resembled appropriate composure, accepting condolences and deflecting questions about her future plans with diplomatic vagueness.

"Quite an unusual situation," observed Lady Pemberton, her tone suggesting that 'unusual' represented a considerable understatement. "I do hope you feel adequately prepared for the responsibilities involved in managing such an estate."

"I'm certain the Earl's confidence was not misplaced," Cecily replied carefully. "Though I'm grateful for any guidance experienced neighbours might offer."

By evening, when the last carriage had departed and the hall returned to its customary quietude, Cecily felt as though she had survived some elaborate theatrical performance in which she had been given the leading role without adequate rehearsal. The funeral marked not merely the Earl's farewell, but her own formal introduction to a world whose rules she was still learning.

Standing in the place where Mr. Cartwright had first pronounced her extraordinary inheritance, she reflected that grief and gratitude made curious companions. She would miss the Earl she had barely known, mourn the conventional life she was leaving behind, and somehow find the courage to embrace whatever extraordinary future lay ahead.

Outside, the peacocks called across the darkening parkland, and somewhere in the distance, church bells marked the evening hour with bronze voices that seemed to bless both endings and beginnings with equal grace.

6

DANGEROUS MAGIC

T he days that followed saw Cecily introduced to Ashcombe's rare collection of people, including the late Earl's chauffeur.

Miles Penrose proved to be a man of perhaps thirty-five years with the quiet competence that spoke of military service and mechanical expertise. He possessed the sort of steady presence that inspired immediate confidence— neither particularly tall nor notably handsome, but radiated reliability in ways that suggested extensive experience managing complex situations.

"Lady Ashcombe," he said, his voice carrying precisely the neutral tone of someone accustomed to dealing with authority whilst maintaining personal dignity. "I served as chauffeur and mechanical maintenance for His late Lordship for three years. I'd like to request permission to continue in that capacity."

"I should be delighted to have you remain, Mr. Penrose," Cecily replied. "Though I should warn you that my requirements might differ from the Earl's. I rather prefer driving myself when possible, and my mechanical knowledge tends towards the... creative."

Miles's expression shifted slightly, revealing what might have been the ghost of a smile. "Begging your pardon, my lady, but I examined your De Dion whilst it was parked yesterday evening. Whoever's maintained her has done excellent work—very innovative solutions to some interesting mechanical challenges."

Cecily felt a flush of pride. "That would be me, actually. Father couldn't afford proper garage fees, so I learned to manage repairs myself."

"Innovation often produces better results than convention, my lady." Miles paused, then continued with the air of someone stating important terms. "If I may, I'd like permission to establish a proper workshop in the estate's coach house. His Lordship preferred all mechanical work conducted off premises, but immediate access to tools would allow better service."

"That sounds eminently practical," Cecily agreed. "Though I should mention that I rather enjoy engine work myself. I hope you wouldn't mind occasional... collaboration?"

Miles's carefully neutral expression finally cracked, revealing genuine surprise and unmistakable approval. "I'd welcome it, my lady. Most folks treat motors like dangerous magic. Pleasant to work with someone who understands they're simply machines requiring proper attention."

As they concluded these straightforward arrangements, Pip emerged from investigating the terrace's decorative urns bearing what appeared to be an extremely valuable bulb in his mouth. He presented this horticultural trophy with obvious pride, his entire body vibrating with self-satisfaction.

"Pip, no!" Cecily exclaimed, but Miles was already chuckling—a warm sound that transformed his serious features entirely.

"Prize tulip bulb, if I'm not mistaken," he observed. "Worth about ten pounds, considering its size."

"Ten pounds?" Cecily stared at her dog in horror. "That's more than some people earn monthly!"

Miles knelt and offered his hand to Pip, who graciously surrendered his horticultural discovery for a thorough ear scratching. "No harm done, my lady. Hardy things, tulip bulbs. Bit of dirt and water, good as new."

Mrs. Fotheringill watched this exchange with an expression suggesting rapid revision of her assessments. Her new mistress discussing mechanics with obvious knowledge, the chauffeur displaying unexpected patience with canine misbehaviour, and molested ten-pound tulip bulbs being considered minor inconveniences clearly required some adjustment of expectations.

"Perhaps," she said carefully, "we should proceed with village introductions before any additional... discoveries... occur."

"Brilliant idea," Elsie agreed, having joined them on the terrace. "Though we should discuss strategy first. Small villages can be tribal about newcomers, particularly those who've suddenly acquired dramatic social elevation."

"What sort of strategy?" Cecily asked, suspecting she wouldn't entirely approve of whatever Elsie had formulated.

"Well, you'll need perfect balance," Elsie explained thoughtfully. "Too humble, and they'll think you're performing false modesty. Too grand, they'll resent you for forgetting your origins. Too familiar, they won't respect your new position. Too formal, they'll believe you've become snobbish."

"That seems rather too many variables to manage simultaneously," Cecily observed.

"Which is precisely why," Mrs. Fotheringill said with surprising warmth, "you'll simply be yourself, my lady. Your father earned tremendous county-wide respect by treating everyone with genuine kindness whilst maintaining appropriate dignity. Those same qualities will serve you well."

Miles nodded approvingly. "His Lordship always said folks could spot false courtesy from considerable distance, but they'd walk through fire for someone who treated them fairly."

"Right then," Cecily said, drawing courage from this pragmatic advice. "Let us meet my new neighbours and discover how spectacularly I might embarrass myself."

"That's the spirit!" Elsie said enthusiastically. "Though do attempt keeping Pip from excavating anything else valuable. At least until we've established your reputation as a responsible landowner."

Pip, apparently sensing his archaeological activities were under discussion, gazed up with innocent expression that had fooled absolutely no one since puppyhood. His tail wagged hopefully, as though volunteering for additional excavation assignments.

"Perhaps," Cecily said, regarding her incorrigible companion, "we should establish an emergency fund for unexpected canine-induced expenses."

∼

As they prepared to venture forth into Little Codding for her first official appearance as Lady Ashcombe, Cecily felt the familiar flutter of nervous excitement she remembered from challenging surgical procedures during the war—equal parts anticipation and terror, seasoned with just enough confidence to navigate whatever unexpected complications might arise.

The morning sun climbed higher over Ashcombe Hall's ancient stones, and somewhere across the countryside, church bells began their call to morning service. Their bronze voices carried familiar authority that reminded her powerfully of Father and his gentle certainty that providence would always provide whatever strength was needed for the tasks at hand.

"Trust in the Lord with all thine heart," she told herself, "and lean not unto thine own understanding."

Drawing her new household around her like armour— Mrs. Fotheringill's steadfast competence, Elsie's unshakeable loyalty, Miles's quiet reliability, and even Pip's enthusiastic chaos—Cecily squared her shoulders and prepared to meet whatever destiny awaited in the village that had somehow, impossibly, become her responsibility.

After all, she'd managed to keep soldiers alive under artillery bombardment with inadequate supplies and impossible conditions. Introducing herself to Little Codding's residents might prove complicated, but surely it couldn't require more courage than she'd already proven herself capable of summoning.

Though given her track record with seemingly simple situations, she rather suspected she shouldn't make assumptions.

The peacocks called from the terrace, their voices carrying across the parkland like exotic heralds announcing the beginning of an adventure that would test everything she'd learned about faith, courage, and the remarkable capacity of ordinary people to rise to extraordinary circumstances when the situation demanded it.

7

PUTTERING INTO LITTLE CODDING

The De Dion puttered down the winding lane towards Little Codding with the sort of mechanical contentment that suggested a well-maintained engine enjoying a pleasant morning constitutional. Cecily gripped the steering wheel with perhaps more determination than the gentle countryside demanded, whilst Elsie maintained a running commentary on the passing scenery from the passenger seat.

"Lovely morning for meeting one's new subjects," Elsie observed cheerfully, adjusting her cloche hat against the autumn breeze that carried the scent of wood smoke and late-blooming roses. "Though I do hope you're prepared for the sort of reception usually reserved for curiosities at travelling fairs."

Pip, installed in the rear seat like a small furry dignitary, had his nose pressed against the window with the intense concentration of someone conducting important reconnaissance. His tail maintained a steady rhythm against the leather upholstery that suggested considerable excitement about the adventure ahead.

"I hardly think of them as subjects," Cecily protested, navigating around a particularly assertive sheep who seemed disinclined to acknowledge automotive right-of-way. "More like... neighbours who happen to live on land I've somehow inherited."

"Neighbours who've been discussing your mysterious elevation since dawn, according to the postman's reports," Elsie replied with characteristic pragmatism. "Mrs. Tuggles apparently held court at the post office until well past closing time yesterday, expounding theories about your inheritance that would put sensation novelists to shame."

As they crested the small hill that overlooked Little Codding, Cecily felt her breath catch slightly. The village spread below them like something from an illustrated children's book—thatched cottages with smoke curling from chimneys, arranged around a green where ancient elm trees cast dappled shadows. The Norman church pointed its charmingly crooked spire heavenward with determined faith, whilst the gentle sound of church bells carried across fields where sheep grazed amongst hedgerows heavy with blackberries.

"It's rather perfect, isn't it?" she murmured, momentarily forgetting her nervousness in favour of genuine appreciation.

"Perfect for hiding all manner of interesting secrets," Elsie agreed, her tone suggesting considerable experience with picturesque villages. "Places this charming usually compensate with appropriately dramatic interpersonal complications."

The De Dion announced their arrival with a gentle puttering that nevertheless managed to attract immediate attention from various quarters. Lace curtains twitched in cottage windows like semaphore flags, a cluster of women near the village green paused their conversation to observe with frank curiosity, and somewhere a cockerel proclaimed territorial authority with the sort of enthusiasm that caused Pip's ears to prick with professional interest.

Cecily brought the motor to a dignified halt beside the village green, where a small crowd had begun to gather with the mysterious efficiency that characterised rural communities whenever anything remotely interesting occurred. She took a steadying breath, drawing courage from Father's voice echoing in her memory: "The Lord your God will be with you wherever you go."

"Right then," she said, more to herself than to Elsie. "Let us discover whether Lady Ashcombe can manage a proper introduction without disgracing herself entirely."

8

CANON BOTT

T heir emergence from the De Dion was observed with the sort of keen attention usually reserved for theatrical performances. Cecily had chosen her outfit carefully—a practical tweed suit in forest green that acknowledged her new status without appearing ostentatious, sturdy walking boots suitable for village exploration, and her grandmother's simple pearl earrings for a touch of understated elegance that spoke of quality rather than ostentation.

Pip's exit from the motor car proved considerably less dignified. Spotting what appeared to be an extremely interesting tabby cat sunning itself on the church steps, he launched himself from the vehicle with the enthusiasm of a cavalry charge, his lead somehow becoming entangled with Cecily's ankle in the process.

What followed could hardly be described as a graceful introduction to her new community. Cecily found herself performing an involuntary dance across the village green whilst Pip pursued his quarry with single-minded determination, the cat responded with appropriate feline outrage, and various villagers watched with expressions ranging from barely concealed amusement to mild alarm.

The chase concluded when both cat and dog somehow managed to wind themselves around the ancient market cross, creating a furry maypole that required diplomatic negotiations between species before order could be restored.

"Well," Elsie observed, helping Cecily untangle herself from the lead whilst Pip sat panting with obvious satisfaction, "that certainly established you as approachable."

"Indeed," came a nervous voice from behind them. "Though I... I do hope Mr. Whiskers hasn't suffered any lasting... that is to say, trauma from the encounter?"

Cecily turned to find herself facing a tall, thin gentleman of perhaps forty years whose clerical collar identified him immediately. Canon Alistair Bott possessed the sort of earnest, scholarly appearance that suggested extensive familiarity with theological texts and rather limited experience with worldly complications involving runaway dogs and territorial cats. His hands trembled slightly as he clutched a leather portfolio to his chest, and his eyes darted anxiously between the assembled villagers as though expecting judgment at any moment.

The collar still bore the creases of recent purchase, and his movements carried the uncertain quality of someone still learning the rhythms of village life. When he spoke, his voice climbed toward nervous heights that suggested someone perpetually on the verge of apologizing for his very existence.

Behind him, Mrs. Tuggles whispered rather audibly to her companion, "Still can't fathom why a gentleman of his... particular background would seek such a modest position in our little village. Just appeared one day with his credentials and references, claiming divine calling to serve amongst us simple folk."

Her companion nodded gravely. "And coming so soon after dear Reverend Ashcombe's passing, when the parish was still mourning properly. Almost unseemly haste, if you ask me. Makes one wonder what circumstances might drive a man to seek... refuge in such quiet corners."

Canon Bott's complexion paled further at these barely concealed observations, his grip tightening on the portfolio as though it contained secrets requiring protection. A bead of perspiration formed on his brow despite the cool autumn air.

"Canon Bott, it is nice to see you again after the Earl's funeral, I apologise that we were not able to be properly introduced there," Cecily said warmly, extending her hand whilst noting how the man's nervousness seemed to intensify under communal scrutiny. "How delightful to properly meet you. I do hope you've found the vicarage comfortable since you moved in? I know Father's old study can be rather overwhelming with all those theological volumes."

His relief at her gracious tone was palpable, the tension visibly draining from his shoulders as he realized he was speaking to someone who wouldn't judge his circumstances.

"You are… extraordinarily kind. The house still holds so much of your dear father's presence. I often feel as though I'm merely... keeping it warm for worthier occupants. And you are, of course, the... well, we're all most... what I mean to say is, congratulations on your inheritance, Lady Ashcombe."

The poor man's obvious discomfort with her sudden elevation was rather touching. Cecily smiled with the gentle warmth she'd learned during years of putting nervous parishioners at ease in Father's study.

"Please, do call me Miss Ashcombe, or simply Cecily, if you prefer. I may have inherited grand titles, but I haven't forgotten that I'm still a vicar's daughter at heart."

Canon Bott's relief was immediately visible, his shoulders relaxing as though she'd lifted a considerable burden. "That's... that's extraordinarily kind of you to... I confess, I've been rather anxious about proper protocols and...

well, my predecessor was so universally beloved, and now with your elevation to such... it's all rather above my usual experience with parish... that is to say, social hierarchies."

"Father always maintained that kindness was the finest protocol," Cecily replied warmly. "Though I should mention that Pip has developed rather strong opinions about cats, so perhaps we should arrange supervised introductions between him and Mr. Whiskers in future."

As if summoned by this diplomatic suggestion, Pip chose that precise moment to discover Canon Bott's coat pocket, from which protruded what appeared to be folded papers covered in handwriting. With the efficiency of an accomplished pickpocket operating during rush hour at Victoria Station, Pip liberated these documents and began what could only be described as an enthusiastic literary critique involving considerable slobber.

"My sermon notes!" Canon Bott exclaimed, diving rather ungracefully to rescue his papers from canine editorial review. "Oh dear, I do hope they're not... that is, they're not particularly... oh mercy me!"

Cecily helped gather the scattered pages, noting with considerable interest that they appeared to contain dramatically more sensational content than typical Sunday sermons. References to "mysterious murders most foul," "suspicious circumstances in the conservatory," and "the butler's guilty conscience exposed at last" seemed rather advanced theological concepts.

"Research materials for my... my private writing," Canon Bott explained, his face flushing crimson whilst he attempted to restore order to his papers. "I find that one requires certain... diversions from purely ecclesiastical pursuits, you understand."

"How absolutely fascinating!" Cecily exclaimed with genuine enthusiasm. "I had no idea you wrote fiction. What manner of stories?"

"Oh, merely small... that is to say, nothing of particular literary merit... well, murder mysteries, actually," he admitted, his voice dropping to nearly a whisper as though confessing participation in something vaguely scandalous. "Published under a pseudonym, you understand, Silas Bellweather, but please don't divulge that to anyone as I prefer to keep it secret. I do hope you don't find such pursuits inappropriate for someone in my... my position?"

"On the contrary, I think it sounds absolutely delightful," Cecily assured him with genuine warmth. "Father always maintained that using one's imagination constructively was a gift to be treasured and developed. I should love to read one of your stories sometime."

Canon Bott's expression suggested she'd just offered him the keys to paradise. Before he could manage an appropriately grateful response, their conversation was interrupted by the approach of a formidable woman whose bearing suggested she intended to conduct some form of official village business with considerable efficiency.

"Canon Bott," she announced in a voice that carried the sort of natural authority that brooked absolutely no contradiction whilst remaining perfectly polite, "perhaps we might properly acknowledge our distinguished visitor in her new capacity?"

The woman appeared to be somewhere in her fifties, possessed of the sort of imposing presence that managed grand households and organised church fêtes with equal competence. Her navy dress was impeccably tailored in the latest fashion, her steel-grey hair arranged with military precision beneath a sensible hat, and her sharp dark eyes missed absolutely nothing of social or practical importance.

"Of course, Mrs... Mrs. Tuggles," Canon Bott stammered, his nervousness returning immediately in the face of such organised efficiency. "Though naturally we all know... that is to say, we're all adjusting to... well, to Miss Cecily's remarkable elevation in circumstances."

Mrs. Tuggles executed a curtsey that struck precisely the right note between appropriate respect for inherited rank and the familiar affection of someone who'd watched Cecily grow up in the vicarage.

"Lady Ashcombe," she said with careful emphasis on the new title, her tone carrying both warmth and a slight adjustment to their changed relationship. "We're all terribly curious about your plans for the estate, naturally. It's rather extraordinary, isn't it, seeing our own dear vicar's daughter transformed into the lady of the manor. Your dear father would have been so proud, though I suspect he's having quite a chuckle about it all from heaven."

"Thank you so very much. I confess I never imagined I'd be meeting with old friends in quite such... elevated circumstances." Cecily glanced around the village green, where various residents continued their discreet observation whilst pretending to conduct normal daily business. "I do hope I might continue the tradition of good relations between the Hall and the village, despite the rather unusual nature of my inheritance."

"I'm quite certain you'll find everyone most accommodating," Mrs. Tuggles replied, though her tone diplomatically suggested this accommodation would depend considerably on Cecily's future behaviour and decisions. "Though I should perhaps mention that Lord Oswald Crowthorne called at the post office yesterday afternoon, making certain... inquiries about estate matters."

The name fell into their conversation rather like a stone dropping into previously still water. Canon Bott's expression grew notably uncomfortable, his papers rustling nervously in his hands, whilst Mrs. Tuggles watched Cecily's reaction with the sharp attention of someone accustomed to reading people's true feelings beneath polite social expressions.

"I see," Cecily replied carefully, maintaining her composure whilst noting the sudden tension. "Was he inquiring about anything in particular?"

"Legal matters, primarily. The validity of inheritance documents, procedures for contesting wills, precedents for similar situations..." Mrs. Tuggles' tone remained diplomatically neutral whilst conveying significant information about Lord Oswald's probable intentions. "He seemed rather... surprised by recent developments regarding the estate's disposition."

Before Cecily could formulate an appropriately diplomatic response to this concerning intelligence, a thunderous voice bellowed across the green with enough volume to startle roosting birds from the church eaves and cause several sheep in adjacent fields to pause their grazing.

9

CAPTAIN TUGGLES

"**A**hoy there! Fresh crew reporting for duty!"

The voice belonged to a man of perhaps seventy years who approached with a distinctive rolling gait that suggested either extensive nautical experience or the sort of artificial leg that required careful navigation across uneven terrain. His weathered face, bronzed by decades of outdoor exposure, was dominated by an impressive white beard that would have done credit to Neptune himself, and his bearing radiated the sort of confidence usually associated with men accustomed to command during challenging circumstances.

"Oh, do stop being so dramatic, Cyril," Mrs. Tuggles said with the resigned affection of someone who'd spent decades managing maritime reminiscences. "My husband, as you know, was briefly in the Royal Navy."

"Briefly?" the Captain roared, clearly having overheard this casual dismissal of his distinguished naval career. "Fifteen years aboard His Majesty's finest vessels, sailing everything from the Mediterranean to the Indian Ocean! Saw action at Jutland, served under Admiral Beatty himself during the most crucial naval engagement of the war!"

"Yes, dear," Mrs. Tuggles replied with the patient tone of someone who'd heard these tales extensively catalogued on numerous previous occasions. "Well, Captain, this is Lady Ashcombe, though I rather suspect you remember her better as little Cecily from the vicarage."

Captain Tuggles swept off his cap with theatrical flourish worthy of the Royal Opera House, revealing a perfectly bald head that gleamed in the morning sunlight like a polished cannon ball.

"Good Lord! Young Cecily! Though I suppose I should say Lady Ashcombe now, shouldn't I?" His eyes twinkled with genuine delight as he took in her transformed circumstances. "Bless my buttons, I can still remember when you were no taller than a ship's capstan, following your dear father about the village like a devoted midshipman! And now look at you—inherited a fine estate! Your father would have been bursting with pride."

"Thank you, Captain Tuggles. Though I confess I'm still adjusting to the considerable responsibilities involved."

"Absolute nonsense! Running an estate is nothing compared to commanding a battle cruiser in heavy seas with German destroyers bearing down on your position," the Captain declared with magnificent confidence. "Simply requires proper organisation, firm discipline, and the occasional strategic retreat when circumstances demand tactical reassessment. Why, I remember teaching you those very principles when you were barely old enough to tie your own shoe laces!"

"The Captain's extensive naval experience provides him with... unique perspectives on most civilian situations," Mrs. Tuggles observed with diplomatic understatement.

"Indeed! Why, I distinctly recall during the Battle of Jutland, Admiral Beatty himself consulted me about tactical approaches when facing superior enemy forces. 'Tuggles,' he said, standing right there on the bridge whilst shells exploded around us, 'what's your professional assessment of our strategic options?' And I replied without hesitation—"

"Perhaps," Mrs. Tuggles interrupted gently but with unmistakable finality, "we might save the detailed maritime reminiscences for later? I believe Lady Ashcombe was hoping to visit with various other village members during her visit."

Cecily found herself rather charmed by the Captain's enthusiasm, whatever liberties he might be taking with historical accuracy. "Actually, I should be delighted to hear about your naval experiences sometime, Captain. Father always maintained that people's stories were treasures worth preserving."

Captain Tuggles positively beamed with delight, his weathered face creasing into smile lines that suggested years of laughter. "Excellent! Capital attitude! I've accumulated tales that would curl your hair—adventures with Barbary pirates off Gibraltar, mysterious cargo runs to Constantinople during delicate diplomatic missions, the time I shared Napoleon brandy with a Russian countess who may or may not have been working as an international spy..."

"All absolutely factual, I'm completely certain," Mrs. Tuggles commented dryly whilst shooting her husband a look that suggested certain editorial restraints might be advisable. "Now then, Lady Ashcombe, perhaps we should say hello to the other ladies? We were just discussing final arrangements for Sunday's harvest festival."

She gestured towards a small cluster of women who'd been conducting their own animated conversation beneath the elm trees, with frequent meaningful glances towards Cecily's group. They approached with the sort of coordinated precision that suggested extensive practice in village social protocols and collective decision-making.

"The Wednesday Circle," Mrs. Tuggles explained as they drew near with obvious purpose. "Our unofficial organising committee for community events, charitable activities, and general village welfare coordination."

The Wednesday Circle proved to consist of four women whose ages ranged from perhaps fifty to seventy-something, each possessing the sort of determined respectability that characterised village social leadership. They were introduced as Mrs. Petunia Stirk (former opera singer), Mrs. Dorothy Brambling (wife of the largest local farmer and mother of six accomplished children), Miss Agatha Plunkett (retired governess whose spine remained ramrod straight despite her years), and Mrs. Violet Crimp (wife of the philosophising local grave digger, whose earth-stained hands spoke of extensive gardening expertise).

"Lady Ashcombe," Mrs. Stirk announced in a voice that still carried traces of theatrical training, "we're simply dying to know about your plans for the estate. His late Lordship was rather... reclusive in recent years."

"I'm still learning about proper estate management myself," Cecily admitted with honest humility. "Though I hope to maintain good employment for the tenant farmers and household staff whilst perhaps modernising certain aspects of operations that might benefit everyone involved."

"Modernising?" Miss Plunkett inquired with the curiosity of someone who'd spent decades educating young people, her tone suggesting possible reservations about change in general and newfangled ideas in particular.

"Nothing dramatically revolutionary," Cecily assured her hastily. "Perhaps improving worker housing conditions, updating some agricultural techniques that might increase productivity, that sort of practical enhancement rather than wholesale alteration of traditional methods."

The ladies exchanged meaningful glances that suggested this answer met with qualified approval, though Cecily suspected she'd be subject to ongoing careful evaluation regarding any actual modernising efforts and their effects on established village life.

"And what about Lord Oswald?" Mrs. Brambling asked with the straightforward directness of someone accustomed to practical farming concerns and little patience for diplomatic evasion. "We understand he's rather... disappointed with recent inheritance developments."

Before Cecily could formulate an appropriate response, Pip announced his return to the conversation by emerging from behind the market cross bearing what appeared to be someone's knitting project trailing from his mouth like colourful wool spaghetti. His expression radiated enormous pride in this latest acquisition.

"That's my unfinished scarf!" Mrs. Crimp exclaimed with maternal outrage, diving to rescue her handiwork from further enthusiastic canine assistance. "I was sitting here earlier, working on the cable pattern..."

The liberation of Mrs. Crimp's knitting involved a brief but energetic negotiation between human determination and canine possessiveness, eventually resolved when Elsie produced a digestive biscuit from her pocket that Pip deemed considerably more immediately valuable than wool craftsmanship, however expertly executed.

"I do apologise most sincerely," Cecily said, helping untangle the slightly damp but essentially undamaged scarf whilst mentally noting that Pip required additional training regarding appropriate behaviour in polite society. "Pip has developed rather unfortunate habits regarding other people's belongings."

"No lasting harm done," Mrs. Crimp assured her generously, though she eyed Pip with appropriate caution whilst securing her knitting safely beyond reach. "Though perhaps you should know that my husband Jeremiah mentioned seeing some unusual activity around the estate grounds recently."

"Unusual in what way?" Cecily asked, her attention sharpening considerably.

Mrs. Crimp glanced around the assembled group before lowering her voice to conspiratorial levels. "Nighttime visitors, according to his observations. People skulking about the grounds after dark, particularly near the old folly ruins. Jeremiah notices these things, you understand, working in the churchyard as he does during all hours."

"Probably poachers," Captain Tuggles declared with confident naval authority. "Had identical problems during my service posting in India—locals creeping about government compounds at all hours of darkness, up to various forms of unauthorised mischief and petty criminality."

"Or perhaps," Mrs. Stirk suggested with dramatic emphasis worthy of her operatic background, "someone searching for something quite specific. Old estates often harbour secrets that certain interested parties prefer to remain permanently buried."

Canon Bott shifted uncomfortably at this ominous observation, clutching his rescued sermon notes with suddenly nervous energy whilst his eyes darted about as though expecting mysterious figures to emerge from behind convenient trees. His reaction seemed rather excessive for someone merely discussing theoretical trespassers, though Cecily couldn't determine whether this indicated guilty knowledge of specific problems or simply his generally nervous disposition when confronted with potentially dramatic situations.

"Well," she said diplomatically whilst filing away this interesting intelligence, "if anyone notices continued unusual activity, please do let me know immediately.

Estate security is certainly my responsibility now, and I should hate for anyone to feel unsafe."

"Speaking of responsibilities," Mrs. Tuggles announced briskly, evidently deciding the conversation required redirection towards more manageable topics, "you really should visit Marjorie Blight's millinery shop whilst you're in the village today. As you know, she's our local authority on fashion and... other matters of considerable community interest."

The particular way she emphasised "other matters" suggested that Marjorie Blight served additional functions beyond hat-making in the village's complex social ecosystem. Cecily filed this valuable information for future reference whilst noting the general approval her practical approaches to estate management seemed to be generating amongst the Wednesday Circle membership.

"Excellent suggestion. Though perhaps we might visit the pub first? I should like to meet as many villagers as possible during our visit."

The suggestion produced a brief but comprehensive silence amongst the assembled ladies. Mrs. Tuggles' expression suggested Cecily had proposed something not necessarily improper, but certainly unexpected.

"The Gilded Goose," Captain Tuggles said approvingly, apparently unaffected by the ladies' concerns about pub visits. "Excellent establishment! Serves the finest ale in three counties, though I've encountered better rum in Port Royal."

"You've never actually been to the Caribbean, dear," Mrs. Tuggles observed with mild resignation.

THE GILDED GOOSE

The procession towards the Gilded Goose resembled nothing so much as a small but highly interested parade with considerable entertainment value for observing villagers. Cecily and Elsie led the way, followed by the Wednesday Circle maintaining carefully coordinated formation, whilst Captain Tuggles brought up the rear providing authoritative running commentary on strategic considerations involved in approaching unfamiliar but potentially friendly establishments.

Canon Bott trailed somewhat behind the main group, clearly torn between proper ministerial responsibility for his parishioner's moral welfare and equally proper deference to her dramatically elevated social status and obvious determination to proceed regardless of clerical concerns.

Pip trotted alongside the entire procession with obvious satisfaction, having successfully ingratiated himself to the entire village community whilst acquiring fascinating new scents, interesting flavours, and the delightful promise of additional adventures lying immediately ahead.

The Gilded Goose occupied a timber-framed building of considerable but indeterminate age that leaned slightly to one side with the sort of picturesque architectural irregularity that suggested centuries of gradual settling into the surrounding landscape without particular concern for geometric precision. Its painted sign featured a somewhat anatomically improbable goose sporting distinctly golden plumage, and warm lamplight glowed invitingly through diamond-paned windows that promised comfort against autumn's growing chill.

As they approached the entrance, Cecily could hear the comfortable murmur of masculine voices from within— the sort of companionable conversation that characterised village public houses during morning hours when serious local residents gathered for equally serious discussion of agricultural conditions, weather prospects, and community affairs requiring careful analysis.

"Here we go," Elsie murmured quietly. "Into the proverbial lion's den."

"With any luck," Cecily replied, "they'll prove to be reasonably friendly lions."

Though given her recent experiences with assumption-making, she rather suspected she shouldn't rely too heavily on luck alone.

~

The interior of the Gilded Goose proved every bit as welcoming as its exterior promised, though considerably more aromatic than Cecily had anticipated. Ancient oak beams had absorbed decades of pipe tobacco, wood smoke, and properly aged ale, creating an atmosphere that spoke of countless evenings devoted to earnest discussion of matters both parochial and profound.

The morning clientele consisted of half a dozen men whose weathered hands and practical bearing marked them as the backbone of Little Codding's agricultural community. Conversation paused naturally as their small procession entered—not from rudeness, but from the entirely reasonable curiosity that accompanied any deviation from established routine in places where routine formed one of life's more reliable pleasures.

"Well now," announced a voice from behind the bar, belonging to a gentleman whose impressive girth and jovial countenance immediately identified him as the publican. "This be a morning for pleasant surprises. Ladies, gentlemen—and most particularly you, Lady Ashcombe—welcome to the Goose."

Mr. Barnaby Thorne possessed the sort of diplomatic nature that kept village pubs functioning as neutral territory where men of varying opinions could gather without their differences escalating into actual hostilities. His greeting struck precisely the right balance between respect for Cecily's newly elevated position and the comfortable familiarity appropriate to local hospitality.

"Mr. Thorne," Cecily replied warmly, "I'm absolutely delighted to meet you. I've heard the most wonderful things about the Goose, and I was hoping to properly introduce myself to as many villagers as possible."

"Aye, well, you've come to exactly the right establishment for that purpose," observed a lean gentleman seated near the window whose earth-stained clothing and extraordinarily practical boots proclaimed his agricultural calling. "Most of Little Codding finds its way through these doors eventually, particularly when the weather's neither fit for outdoor labour nor domestic harmony."

The assembled men chuckled with comfortable appreciation, the sound of people who understood both farming schedules and matrimonial dynamics with equal expertise.

"Tom Pickering," the farmer continued, rising to offer a respectful nod. "I work the largest holding on estate land —been tenant farmers there nigh on forty years now, my family has. Sorry for the loss of your ma and pa, they were fine folks."

"Thank you, Mr. Pickering," Cecily said, her attention sharpening with genuine interest. "I should very much like to discuss estate matters with the tenant farmers at your earliest convenience. I understand there've been... concerns about certain aspects of land management in recent years?"

A perceptible shift occurred in the pub's atmosphere—not precisely tension, but the sort of careful attention that accompanied discussion of matters affecting the entire community's welfare.

"Aye, well," Tom Pickering said tactfully, "his late Lordship was a good man, none could say otherwise. But perhaps not entirely... current with modern agricultural methods, if you take my meaning, my lady."

"Drainage systems haven't been properly maintained in near a decade," offered another farmer, whose rolled sleeves revealed arms suggesting extensive familiarity with manual labour. "And some of the estate cottages want considerable work before winter sets in proper."

"Then we shall certainly address those issues," Cecily said firmly. "During the war, I learned that practical problems require practical solutions, preferably implemented before they become emergencies threatening everyone's wellbeing."

The exchange of glances amongst the assembled men suggested this approach met with considerably more approval than previous estate management policies had apparently generated.

"Begging your pardon, Lady Ashcombe," Tom Pickering continued carefully, "but there's been talk in the village that Lord Oswald might... that is to say, if he were to challenge your inheritance through the courts..."

"Lord Oswald is perfectly entitled to pursue whatever legal recourse he considers appropriate," Cecily replied diplomatically, though her tone conveyed no particular anxiety about such challenges. "However, I can assure you that all inheritance documents are completely proper and legally binding. The Earl's solicitors were extraordinarily thorough in their preparations."

Before anyone could pursue this potentially delicate topic further, Pip announced his presence by emerging from beneath a corner table bearing what appeared to be someone's partially consumed shepherd's pie balanced precariously in his determined jaws. His expression radiated enormous pride in this culinary appropriation, though his transportation technique suggested urgent need for additional training in proper public house etiquette.

"Pip, absolutely not!" Cecily exclaimed, diving to rescue the unfortunate meal whilst apologising profusely to its legitimate owner—a red-faced gentleman whose initial outrage transformed into reluctant amusement when Pip offered his most charming tail-wagging apology.

"No harm done whatsoever," the man chuckled, accepting Mr. Thorne's immediate offer of replacement refreshment. "Though perhaps that little fellow might benefit from learning proper table manners before his next social engagement, eh?"

The incident served to dissolve remaining formality between Cecily and her acquaintances, establishing her as someone refreshingly unconcerned with artificial dignity when practical matters required immediate attention.

Their departure from the Goose was accompanied by genuine warmth and multiple invitations for future visits, along with promises that various agricultural concerns would be addressed through proper meetings between estate management and tenant representatives.

11

GOOD OLE BLIGHTY

"That went considerably better than I dared hope," Cecily confided to Elsie as they walked toward Marjorie Blight's establishment, located in a charming half-timbered building whose bow windows displayed an impressive array of millinery creations ranging from practical to positively architectural in their ambitious scope.

"The men seemed genuinely pleased with your straightforward approach," Elsie agreed. "Though I suspect the real test lies ahead—village ladies can be considerably more... complex in their social evaluations than farmers discussing drainage problems."

The millinery shop's interior proved a veritable wonderland of feminine fashion, with hats perched on stands like exotic birds displaying various stages of elaborate plumage. Ribbons, feathers, artificial flowers, and other decorative elements created controlled chaos that somehow suggested both artistic creativity and commercial competence.

Marjorie Blight herself emerged from behind a curtained alcove with theatrical timing that spoke of extensive practice in dramatic entrances. She was a woman of perhaps fifty years whose own hat—a magnificent creation involving peacock feathers, silk roses, and what appeared to be a small stuffed bird of indeterminate species—established immediate credentials as someone who approached millinery with absolute seriousness.

"Lady Ashcombe," she announced in cultured tones that overlay rural origins like expensive silk covering sturdy cotton, "how absolutely divine to meet you at last. I have been simply perishing with curiosity ever since news of your remarkable inheritance reached our little community."

Something in her delivery suggested that whilst she might indeed have been dying of curiosity, her feelings about the inheritance itself proved considerably more complicated than simple congratulation.

"Miss Blight," Cecily replied warmly, "your shop is absolutely extraordinary. I've never seen such creative millinery work—each piece tells its own story."

"Oh, you're far too kind. Though I do pride myself on creating hats specifically designed for their wearers' particular... circumstances and requirements." Marjorie's dark eyes studied Cecily with intensity suggesting assessment extending far beyond simple fashion consultation. "I find myself wondering what sort of story your hat might tell, my dear."

Cecily touched her simple cloche self-consciously, suddenly aware that her practical choice appeared rather modest amongst the elaborate creations surrounding them.

"I suppose it would tell a rather straightforward story of someone attempting to navigate unfamiliar territory without making too spectacular a fool of herself."

"Ah, but that's where you're quite mistaken," Marjorie said with a smile that failed to reach her sharp eyes. "Sometimes the most spectacular tales begin with people who insist they're perfectly ordinary. Take your inheritance, for instance—absolutely nothing ordinary about a vicar's daughter suddenly acquiring one of the county's finest estates, particularly when certain... interested parties expected rather different arrangements."

"I understand Lord Oswald was rather disappointed by the Earl's decision," Cecily said diplomatically, noting Majorie grimace at the mention of his Oswald's name.

"Disappointed." Marjorie's laugh held little genuine amusement. "Oh my dear, that's rather like calling the Battle of Waterloo a minor geographical disagreement. Oswald has been counting on inheriting Ashcombe Hall for years—making plans, promising various people certain... considerations once he gained proper control. I fitted him for a hat only yesterday, quite a work of art if I say so myself. Cost him a pretty penny, although I would much prefer a more gentlemanly head for it to sit upon!"

"I see," said Cecily, somewhat taken aback. "Naturally, I understand that my inheritance has created some awkwardness for people who harboured different expectations."

"Yes, one might describe it that way. Oswald has earned quite a reputation here, as I'm sure you are finding out. Though I should warn you, dear, that stirring up old troubles sometimes uncovers things that certain people much prefer to keep buried beneath respectable appearances."

Before Cecily could inquire about the specific nature of these potentially troublesome revelations, Pip discovered a basket of decorative feathers and launched what could only be described as an enthusiastic expedition, resulting in multicoloured plumage scattered across the shop floor like evidence of a very small but very thorough pillow fight.

"Pip, cease that immediately!" Cecily scolded, rushing to prevent further millinery destruction whilst Marjorie observed with an expression suggesting this sort of chaos was precisely what she'd expected from someone whose elevation exceeded her apparent qualifications for managing either estates or terriers.

As Cecily left to return to the manor, she filed away yet another instance of warnings disguised as casual conversation from people who seemed to possess remarkable knowledge about potential estate complications.

12

AN UNEXPECTED VISITOR

The afternoon passed in a whirlwind of domestic preparations whose complexity reinforced Cecily's growing appreciation for Mrs. Fotheringill's organisational competence. The selection of appropriate china, positioning of floral arrangements, coordination of multiple courses requiring precise timing, and establishment of proper seating protocols proved far more involved than her vicarage upbringing had provided preparation for managing.

"I had absolutely no idea that entertaining required such extensive strategic planning," she confided to Elsie whilst contemplating the bewildering array of silverware whose specific purposes remained mysteriously unclear despite Mrs. Fotheringill's patient explanations.

"Think of it rather like organising a field hospital," Elsie suggested practically. "Multiple patients requiring different treatments, limited resources, complex schedules, potentially explosive personalities—exactly the sort of challenge you managed throughout the war with considerable success."

This comparison proved unexpectedly comforting, providing familiar framework for approaching what had seemed overwhelming social complexity. By six o'clock, Cecily felt reasonably confident about providing appropriate hospitality without entirely disgracing either herself or the memory of the previous Earl's entertaining standards.

The guests began arriving punctually at seven, each contributing their distinctive personality to what promised to be an eclectic evening. Dr. Bell appeared first, striding up the front drive with characteristic efficiency whilst carrying what appeared to be her medical bag—apparently she believed in maintaining professional preparedness regardless of social circumstances.

"Cecily," she said warmly, accepting Mrs. Fotheringill's assistance with her coat whilst surveying the entrance hall's arrangements with obvious appreciation. "You've certainly done the old place proud. His late Lordship would be thoroughly pleased with these improvements."

Canon Bott arrived in a flutter of nervous energy, clutching a leather portfolio with protective intensity whilst somehow managing to trip over Pip despite the terrier's position at least three feet from any logical pathway.

"Lady Ashcombe! So tremendously kind of you to... that is to say, absolutely delighted to... I do hope I haven't arrived inappropriately early, though punctuality can sometimes be considered..." His voice trailed into characteristic uncertainty.

"Canon Bott," Cecily interrupted gently, "you're perfectly punctual and absolutely welcome. I see you've brought your manuscript—how exciting!"

Captain and Mrs. Tuggles arrived with perfectly coordinated precision that suggested extensive experience attending social events as a unified command structure. The Captain had dressed in what appeared to be his finest naval-inspired attire, complete with brass buttons gleaming like miniature suns, whilst Mrs. Tuggles wore navy silk that managed both elegance and practicality.

The drawing room conversations flowed with surprising ease. Dr. Bell shared carefully edited wartime tales, Canon Bott discussed his literary pursuits with growing enthusiasm, and Captain Tuggles launched into increasingly elaborate naval adventures whose relationship to actual maritime experience became progressively more creative as the evening progressed.

They were deeply engaged in discussing the challenges of maintaining authentic period detail in historical fiction when the front door's ancient bell announced an unexpected arrival with imperious clanging that suggested someone accustomed to immediate attention regardless of convenience.

Mr. St. John approached the drawing room with unusual haste, his expression conveying significant disapproval of whatever domestic disruption currently required navigation.

"My lady," he announced with carefully controlled professional neutrality, "Lord Oswald Crowthorne has arrived and requests immediate audience regarding matters of... considerable urgency."

The drawing room fell silent with theatrical completeness. Even Pip paused his carpet investigation to regard the butler with alert attention.

Before anyone could discuss protocols for uninvited guests, Lord Oswald Crowthorne swept into the room with dramatic flair. His new hat was a striking creation of deep burgundy velvet with elaborate gold braiding and an ostentatious pheasant feather that swept dramatically across the crown—clearly one of Marjorie Blight's more ambitious millinery efforts.

Despite entering a lady's drawing room in the company of assembled guests, Lord Oswald displayed his characteristic disdain for proper breeding by keeping the fashionable headpiece firmly planted on his head, a breach of elementary social courtesy that spoke volumes about his fundamental disregard for civilized behaviour.

He was a man of perhaps thirty-five years whose bearing proclaimed extensive familiarity with his own importance and considerable impatience with obstacles to achieving his objectives. His evening dress was impeccable in a way that spoke of London tailoring and fashionable attention to detail, though his expression conveyed irritation rather than social pleasure.

"Lady Ashcombe," he said, his tone managing to convey respect for her title whilst somehow suggesting doubt about her qualifications for bearing it, "how... quaint of you to be entertaining the local populace in the family drawing room."

The insult landed with precisely the effect he'd clearly intended, though delivered with sufficient politeness that direct objection would appear churlish.

"Lord Oswald," Cecily replied, "what an unexpected pleasure. May I present Dr. Bell, Canon Bott, and Captain and Mrs. Tuggles?"

Oswald's acknowledgment was perfunctory—brief nods suggesting he considered their presence irrelevant to his immediate purposes and possibly inappropriate for witnessing whatever discussion he intended to pursue.

"Charming," he said dismissively. "Though I wonder if we might discuss certain pressing estate matters somewhat more... privately? These legal complications require attention from people with appropriate breeding and background knowledge."

"I'm quite certain that any estate business can be discussed amongst friends," Cecily replied firmly, her wartime experience providing valuable practice with difficult authority figures. "Unless you'd prefer to schedule a separate meeting at a more mutually convenient time?"

Oswald's eyes narrowed at this diplomatic refusal to be intimidated into private conferences that might prove strategically disadvantageous.

"As you wish. Though I should warn you that the inheritance situation regarding this estate is considerably more... precarious than you may have been led to believe by interested parties."

"Precarious in what fashion?" Cecily inquired politely, though prepared for whatever legal complications he might introduce.

"The Earl's mental capacity during his final months, for instance. Elderly gentlemen suffering from various... afflictions of age often make decisions that fail to reflect their true intentions or the legitimate interests of their established families." His smile held no warmth whatsoever. "Fortunately, English law provides appropriate remedies for such regrettable situations."

"The Earl was in complete possession of his faculties," Cecily said firmly. "Dr. Bell can certainly attest to his mental clarity during recent medical consultations."

"Indeed, I can," Dr. Bell interjected with crisp authority. "His Lordship's mind remained sharp and focused until the day he died. Any suggestion otherwise would be completely inaccurate." Her disdain for Oswald was palpable.

Oswald's expression suggested that medical contradictions were unwelcome complications rather than authoritative clarifications.

"How... fortuitous that the attending physician supports the highly irregular inheritance that elevates her personal friend to possession of valuable properties originally intended for legitimate family members," he observed with a tone that managed to imply impropriety without making directly actionable accusations.

The drawing room's temperature seemed to drop several degrees as everyone registered the implications of this carefully phrased insult.

Mr. St. John's perfectly timed entrance announcing dinner provided temporary relief from escalating hostilities, though his expression suggested profound awareness of current social complications.

13

TROUBLE BREWING

The meal that followed became an exercise in diplomatic navigation that would have challenged experienced ambassadors. Mrs. Fotheringill had outdone herself with seasonal courses demonstrating both culinary skill and appropriate presentation, though these efforts were somewhat undermined by persistent tension generated by the unwelcome guest's presence and obvious dissatisfaction.

Oswald's observations over dinner were clearly designed to undermine Cecily's confidence whilst highlighting his superior familiarity with estate management and aristocratic protocols, although his strategy proved less effective than anticipated, succeeding primarily in alienating everyone present. His face bore the telltale flush of someone who had embraced liquid refreshment with considerably more enthusiasm than prudence might have advised. In his increasingly lubricated state, his demeanour shifted toward what he clearly considered incendiary reminiscence.

"Ah, this takes me back to the lively days when I used to host my London friends at the Hall during shooting season," he began with affected nostalgia. "Such spirited gatherings we had—young gentlemen of proper breeding, you understand, not the sort of... rustic entertainment apparently favoured nowadays."

Flicking the feather on his headpiece, his gaze swept the table with obvious condescension before continuing. "Of course, the village was considerably more... accommodating in those days. Local society understood the natural order of things. Young ladies knew their place, and there was none of this modern nonsense about women pursuing inappropriate professions or forgetting their domestic destinies."

Dr Bell's fork paused midway to her mouth, her expression barely concealed mounting rage.

"I do recall one particularly amusing incident," Oswald continued with malicious pleasure, "when certain village... shall we say, beauties... competed quite enthusiastically for the attention of visiting gentlemen. Such delightful confusion over proper social boundaries! Though I must say, ruffling a few village petticoats provided considerable entertainment for everyone involved."

Mrs. Fotheringill's face flushed scarlet, her hands trembling slightly as she attempted to continue serving whilst clearly struggling with outrage at this casual dismissal of local women's reputations.

"Naturally, such diversions were perfectly innocent," Oswald added with a smirk that suggested precisely the opposite. "Though some of the local families seemed to develop rather... elevated expectations about their daughters' prospects. Most amusing, really, watching them flutter about society events hoping to catch the eye of their social superiors."

"Lord Oswald," Dr Bell said with icy precision, "I find your recollections both offensive and entirely inappropriate for polite company."

"Oh, my dear Doctor," Oswald replied with exaggerated surprise, "surely someone in your... unconventional profession understands that men of the world occasionally require entertainment beyond the tedious constraints of village propriety? Though I suppose your particular lonely circumstances prevent you from fully appreciating such masculine pursuits."

The silence that followed Oswald's crude remarks stretched taut as a bowstring. Dr. Bell's knuckles had gone white where she gripped her wine glass, the crystal trembling slightly with barely contained fury. Mrs. Fotheringill stood frozen by the sideboard, her face cycling through shades of mortification and rage that spoke to deeply personal offense taken.

"Lord Oswald," Cecily said, her voice carrying the steel she had learned during wartime when dealing with impossible superiors, "I believe you have said quite enough for one evening. Your observations about the local community are both inaccurate and deeply offensive to people who have shown me nothing but kindness and respect."

Oswald's wine-flushed face split into a condescending smile. "How refreshingly naive. Though I suppose someone of your... limited social experience... might find it difficult to distinguish between genuine respect and the sort of deference people show when they hope to benefit from sudden elevations in fortune."

"That's quite enough," Captain Tuggles interjected with military authority, his naval bearing suggesting he'd dealt with insubordinate officers before. "You're a guest in this lady's house, sir, and your conduct is entirely inappropriate."

"Guest?" Oswald laughed harshly. "I hardly consider myself a guest in what should rightfully be my own ancestral home. Though I suppose the current... occupant... deserves some credit for attempting to play hostess with such charming rusticity."

The insult hung in the air like smoke from a fired cannon. Even Pip seemed to sense the hostile atmosphere, retreating to a safe position beneath Cecily's chair while maintaining watchful surveillance of the increasingly volatile nobleman, who had begun dabbing at his perspiring forehead with his napkin despite the drawing room's comfortable temperature.

Mrs. Fotheringill quietly began clearing the final course with movements that suggested she was exercising considerable self-control to avoid more dramatic responses to Oswald's offensive commentary. Her professional dedication to completing service despite personal outrage spoke volumes about both her character and her opinion of the unwelcome guest who had so thoroughly poisoned the evening's atmosphere.

"I think we might retire to the drawing room," interjected Cecily, hoping to diffuse the situation before someone— quite possibly herself—said something that would require either an apology or a duel.

"Capital notion," declared Mrs. Tuggles with the sort of enthusiasm typically reserved for announcing tactical retreats from untenable positions. "And may I propose we toast the true Lady of the house—someone who actually knows how to behave like one."

Her pointed glance at Oswald could have cut glass, whilst her emphasis on 'true' and 'actually' managed to deliver a devastating critique of his conduct without uttering a single directly objectionable word.

"Perhaps we might indeed adjourn," Cecily agreed, recognizing that separating the warring parties before someone resorted to actual violence represented sound strategic thinking. "I believe we could all benefit from a change of atmosphere."

14

A MOST UNFORTUNATE TOAST

As the party rose from the dining table with audible relief, Oswald swayed slightly—whether from wine consumption or mounting fury remained unclear, though both seemed equally dangerous to the evening's remaining civility. His burgundy hat had shifted askew during dinner, the ostentatious pheasant feather now drooping in a manner that somehow made his entire appearance seem both ridiculous and vaguely menacing.

"Drawing room refreshments, my lady?" Mr. St. John inquired with professional neutrality, though his expression conveyed complete awareness of the social battlefield his dining room had become.

"Yes, please arrange port and brandy for the gentlemen," Cecily replied, grateful for any activity that might redirect attention from Oswald's increasingly volatile presence.

The migration to the drawing room proceeded with the careful formality of diplomatic negotiations, everyone positioning themselves with obvious strategic consideration. Dr. Bell claimed a chair near the fireplace with clear sight lines to all exits, Captain Tuggles established himself at a central position suggesting military preparedness for rapid response to developing situations, and Canon Bott clutched his manuscript portfolio like a shield whilst seeking refuge near the bookshelf.

Oswald, meanwhile, surveyed the room with proprietorial satisfaction that suggested he considered this temporary retreat rather than acknowledgment of his thoroughly inappropriate conduct.

"Charming arrangements," he commented with false appreciation whilst examining the furniture with calculating eyes. "Though naturally certain pieces will require... updating... once proper ownership is established."

Cecily moved to the sideboard where Mrs. Fotheringill was hastily arranging decanters with appropriate glasses, her usually composed demeanor betraying lingering agitation as she positioned the crystal with sharp, precise movements that spoke of barely contained emotions. Despite her evident distress over Oswald's offensive remarks, she maintained her professional dedication to proper service, though her hands trembled slightly as she prepared the necessary refreshments for what had become a thoroughly uncomfortable social gathering.

Cecily was determined to conclude the evening on a positive note despite Oswald's continuing presence.

"I should like to propose a toast," she announced, lifting the port decanter with ceremonial gravity, "to the memory of his late Lordship, who brought us all together through his kindness and wisdom."

The guests received this suggestion with obvious approval, rising to accept glasses whilst murmuring agreement about honouring their departed host's memory.

As Cecily moved among her guests serving port, Oswald stepped forward with deliberate authority.

"I shall require you to pour mine personally," he announced with the sort of commanding tone that brooked no argument. "Family precedence, you understand—certain proprieties must be observed."

Something in his manner suggested this request carried significance beyond simple etiquette, though Cecily couldn't fathom his reasoning. She complied with his demand, carefully pouring port directly from the crystal decanter into his glass whilst he watched with intense attention.

"To the Earl," Cecily said, raising her glass with genuine emotion. "May his memory remind us all that true nobility lies in service to others rather than personal advantage."

The toast was drunk with appropriate solemnity, though Oswald's participation seemed notably reluctant compared to the genuine warmth displayed by other guests.

"Excellent port," Captain Tuggles observed with professional appreciation. "Reminds me of exceptional vintage we shared during diplomatic celebrations aboard HMS Indomitable whilst anchored off Gibraltar—"

His reminiscence was interrupted by a sharp gasp from Oswald, whose complexion had suddenly transformed from superior displeasure to something approaching genuine alarm. The port glass slipped from nerveless fingers to shatter against the hearth stones whilst his other hand clutched dramatically at his throat.

"I say," he managed to croak before his knees buckled and he collapsed onto the Persian rug with theatrical completeness that would have impressed touring Shakespeare companies.

The drawing room erupted into immediate chaos as guests responded with varying degrees of helpful confusion. Canon Bott dropped his portfolio and rushed forward with obvious concern, Captain Tuggles bellowed maritime commands about securing the patient whilst providing adequate ventilation, and Pip contributed enthusiastic barking.

Dr. Bell reached Oswald first, her medical training overriding personal animosity as she knelt to conduct rapid vital sign assessment.

"Send for my medical bag immediately," she ordered calmly whilst checking pulse and breathing. "And ask Mrs. Fotheringill for hot water and clean towels."

Cecily hurried to comply whilst her mind raced through possible explanations for this dramatic development. Oswald had seemed perfectly healthy, if somewhat erratic. Despite his disagreeable personality, his sudden collapse suggested serious medical complications rather than social awkwardness overwhelming his capacity for civilised behaviour.

"How is he?" she asked anxiously, returning to find Dr. Bell conducting increasingly concerned examination.

"Not well," Dr. Bell replied grimly, moving from pulse points to examining Oswald's eyes with professional focus. "His pulse is extremely rapid and weak, pupils are dilated, breathing is becoming increasingly laboured."

She paused to look directly at Cecily with profound gravity. "I believe Lord Oswald is suffering a severe cardiac episode."

"A heart attack?" Canon Bott repeated faintly, his complexion assuming a greenish tinge that suggested his fictional murder research had provided insufficient preparation for actual medical emergencies in domestic settings.

"The symptoms suggest cardiac arrest," Dr. Bell confirmed with professional certainty, though her expression remained troubled. "Though the sudden onset and severity are... unusual for a man of his age. I believe he may have been poisoned."

Despite Dr. Bell's obvious competence and genuine efforts to provide treatment, Oswald's condition deteriorated with alarming rapidity. His breathing became progressively more laboured until it ceased entirely despite all resuscitation attempts.

"I'm very sorry," she said finally, sitting back with practised gravity that accompanied delivering tragic news. "There's nothing more I can do. Lord Oswald is dead."

The quiet that followed was profound and terrible, broken only by the mantelpiece clock's ticking whilst everyone absorbed the shocking transformation of their social evening into something considerably more serious and dangerous.

"Dead? Oh my!" Canon Bott whispered. "But surely... that is, people don't simply... not from drinking port during perfectly civilised social gatherings..." His eyes shifted from Oswald's still form to Cecily's face, lingering there with obvious unease. He swallowed hard as his gaze moved pointedly between the shattered crystal and the woman who had personally poured the fatal drink. His mouth opened as if to speak, then closed again, the unfinished words hanging in the air.

Cecily stared at the shattered glass remains whilst struggling to process the impossible reality that someone had died in her drawing room after drinking port she had personally served. Pip, sensing magnitude beyond his comprehension, pressed firmly against Cecily's legs in a gesture of canine solidarity that was both comforting and utterly inadequate to address the enormity of her current predicament.

Outside, wind rattled the windows with increasing intensity, and somewhere in the distance church bells began tolling the hour with bronze voices that echoed like a funeral dirge across Ashcombe Hall's ancient grounds.

As she looked around at the shocked faces of her guests and the still form of Lord Oswald Crowthorne lying on her Persian rug, Cecily couldn't help wondering if her faith would prove sufficient to navigate the treacherous waters that now lay ahead.

15

CONSTABLE FENCHURCH

The arrival of Constable Percy Fenchurch proved both inevitable and thoroughly inadequate to the gravity of their situation. He pedalled up the drive on his official bicycle with considerable determination, though his subsequent dismount suggested that dignity and urgency were mutually exclusive concepts in his professional repertoire. His bicycle clips remained stubbornly attached to his trouser legs as he approached the front door, creating a peculiar waddle that rather undermined the authoritative impression he was clearly attempting to project.

Constable Fenchurch was a man whose earnest desire to serve justice was consistently undermined by an unfortunate tendency to approach complex situations armed with nothing more than good intentions and a well-thumbed copy of "Police Procedures for Rural Districts." His uniform, whilst impeccably maintained by what one could only assume was a very patient wife, somehow managed to appear simultaneously too large and too small, creating the impression of someone perpetually growing into responsibilities that remained stubbornly beyond his current capabilities.

"Lady Ashcombe!" he announced, breathing heavily as he navigated the entrance hall whilst fumbling with notebook, pencil, and what appeared to be a small evidence collection bag that seemed more suited to gathering mushrooms than preserving criminal evidence. "I came immediately upon receiving word from young Timothy about... that is to say, a possible situation requiring official... though I hardly dared hope it was merely a misunderstanding..."

His voice trailed off as he took in the solemn faces of the assembled household, the lingering tension in the air, and Mrs. Fotheringill's expression of grim confirmation that suggested no misunderstanding would provide easy resolution to whatever crisis had summoned him from his comfortable village routine.

"Constable Fenchurch," Cecily said gently, recognising that the poor man needed careful handling to maintain what remained of his professional composure, "I'm afraid we have indeed had a death. Lord Oswald Crowthorne collapsed during dinner, and Dr. Bell believes he may have been poisoned."

The word 'poisoned' struck Constable Fenchurch with all the subtlety of a church bell tolling directly inside his head. His ruddy complexion assumed a decidedly greenish tinge that suggested his previous experience with serious crime had been conducted entirely through theoretical study of police manuals rather than practical application in actual criminal situations.

"Poisoned," he repeated faintly, his voice climbing toward panic whilst his hands began an elaborate fumbling routine with his notebook that resulted in loose pages scattering across Mrs. Fotheringill's beautifully polished entrance hall like official confetti. "That is to say... deliberate harm... though surely not in Little Codding... not during a proper dinner party..."

"Most unfortunately, yes," Dr. Bell confirmed briskly, emerging from the drawing room with the crisp efficiency that had made her legendary among battlefield surgeons who possessed neither time nor patience for delicate sensibilities. "Death occurred despite immediate medical intervention, and the symptoms were entirely consistent with cardiac arrest brought on by alkaloid poisoning."

Constable Fenchurch stared at her with the expression of someone discovering that years of theoretical preparation proved woefully inadequate for managing actual emergencies involving actual corpses and actual criminal activity requiring actual detective work.

"Dr. Bell," he managed, clearly struggling to reconcile his comfortable assumptions about village life with the stark reality of deliberate murder occurring in his jurisdiction, "you're absolutely certain we're dealing with... with intentional poisoning rather than, perhaps, natural causes? Or possibly accidental consumption of something inadvertently... that is to say..."

"Quite certain, Constable. The progression of symptoms, the rapidity of onset, the complete failure of standard treatment protocols—all entirely consistent with deliberate administration of poison in sufficient quantity to ensure fatal results." Dr. Bell's clinical precision left no room for hopeful alternative explanations that might restore everyone's faith in village tranquillity.

The definitive nature of this diagnosis appeared to overwhelm Constable Fenchurch's capacity for denial regarding serious criminal activity disrupting his previously peaceful domain.

"Murder," he whispered, apparently requiring considerable effort to pronounce such an extraordinary word in connection with actual circumstances requiring his professional attention. "Deliberate, premeditated murder. Here. In Ashcombe Hall. During what should have been a perfectly civilised dinner party."

"I'm afraid so," Cecily confirmed sympathetically, recognising that the poor man's entire worldview was undergoing rapid and uncomfortable adjustment.

"Though I should point out that everyone present has remained here awaiting your arrival. No one has left the premises or had opportunity to dispose of evidence."

This consideration seemed to provide some small comfort to the overwhelmed Constable, who began rallying his professional training with visible effort whilst attempting to project competent authority over circumstances that clearly exceeded his previous experience.

"Right. Yes. Quite proper procedure." He retrieved his scattered papers with renewed determination whilst consulting his notebook for appropriate protocols. "Now then, I shall need to examine the... the scene of the crime, interview all witnesses systematically, and preserve relevant evidence for subsequent examination by qualified authorities."

His transformation from overwhelmed village policeman to confident investigator proved somewhat less convincing than he'd clearly hoped, though his genuine desire to perform his duties properly was both touching and encouraging given the alternatives.

Dr. Bell led the small procession back to the drawing room, where Lord Oswald's body remained precisely as he'd fallen. Someone—undoubtedly Mrs. Fotheringill— had covered him with a pristine white sheet whilst maintaining the dignity appropriate to even thoroughly disagreeable deceased persons, and had carefully removed Oswald's hat and placed it beside his body, though the shattered crystal and dark wine stains spreading across the Persian rug provided stark evidence of the evening's shocking conclusion.

Constable Fenchurch approached the scene with obvious trepidation.

"Right then," he announced with forced authority, consulting his notes for proper investigative procedures. "First, we must identify and preserve the murder weapon. Which was, according to witness testimony, the port wine served from that specific decanter?"

He gestured toward the sideboard with accusatory certainty, apparently relieved to identify a tangible object requiring official attention rather than abstract concepts like motive and opportunity that promised considerably more complexity.

"Actually," Dr. Bell interjected with diplomatic precision, "we cannot yet determine whether the poison was introduced into the port supply generally, added to Lord Oswald's specific glass, or administered through some entirely different method. The decanter contents require proper analysis before we can establish the precise delivery mechanism."

This professional reality clearly frustrated Constable Fenchurch's desire for straightforward evidence supporting uncomplicated explanations that would minimise the actual detective work required for successful case resolution.

"But surely," he protested with the logic of someone seeking simple solutions to complex problems, "if the gentleman died immediately after consuming port wine, then obviously the port contained the poison? Elementary deduction, one might reasonably conclude."

"One might," Dr. Bell agreed diplomatically, "though the symptoms appeared several minutes after consumption, and poisoning could have been accomplished through numerous alternative methods requiring considerably more sophisticated analysis than initial appearances might suggest."

The prospect of sophisticated analysis involving considerably more detective work than straightforward evidence examination clearly exceeded Constable Fenchurch's current comfort level with criminal investigation procedures.

Meanwhile, Pip had begun conducting his own systematic examination of the crime scene with characteristic thoroughness, his sensitive nose detecting fascinating scents that apparently required immediate and comprehensive investigation. His exploration proved both methodical and unfortunately disruptive to whatever official evidence preservation protocols Constable Fenchurch was attempting to implement.

"That animal," the Constable observed with mounting anxiety whilst watching Pip's enthusiastic investigation, "is systematically disturbing potential evidence. Shouldn't someone restrain the creature before it compromises important forensic materials?"

"Pip," Cecily called gently, recognising that canine assistance was probably not included in standard police procedure manuals, "perhaps you might investigate areas that don't involve walking directly through the location of Lord Oswald's final moments?"

Pip responded to this suggestion by discovering something extraordinarily interesting beneath the armchair nearest the fireplace. His enthusiastic excavation, accompanied by excited whimpering and vigorous tail wagging, eventually produced what appeared to be a small silver object that glinted appealingly in the lamplight.

"What has he uncovered now?" Dr. Bell wondered, moving to examine Pip's discovery whilst Constable Fenchurch fumbled through his pockets for appropriate evidence collection materials.

The object proved to be an ornate silver pillbox bearing elaborate engraved initials that remained clearly visible despite obvious age and extensive handling. The craftsmanship suggested expensive London manufacture, and the monogramming displayed the sort of ornate styling popular several decades previous.

"Whose initials are these?" Cecily asked, accepting the pillbox from Dr. Bell's careful examination whilst trying to decipher the elaborate script. "They appear to be... A.B., though the engraving style makes definitive identification somewhat challenging."

A profound silence greeted this discovery, as everyone present began mentally cataloguing their fellow dinner guests for individuals whose names corresponded to those particular initials.

"A.B.," Canon Bott repeated nervously, his voice climbing toward genuine panic whilst his complexion assumed an unhealthy pallor. "But surely that's merely coincidental... though certainly someone may have dropped some personal belongings accidentally during the confusion following Lord Oswald's collapse..."

"Anthony Bott," Mrs. Tuggles said quietly, her expression grave with uncomfortable implications. "Those are your initials, Canon. And I believe I've seen you with that pillbox before."

Canon Bott's face grew even paler as all eyes turned toward him. "Oh my, yes, yes, well... that is mine, I'm afraid. I must have dropped it during the shock of poor Oswald keeling over as he did. Quite understandable under such distressing circumstances, surely?"

Constable Fenchurch seized upon this concrete evidence with obvious relief, carefully wrapping the pillbox in his handkerchief whilst making elaborate notes about its discovery and potential significance to the criminal investigation.

"Excellent progress!" he announced with renewed confidence that suggested physical evidence provided welcome relief from theoretical detective work. "Tangible proof linking a specific individual to the crime scene through personal property. Now we're proceeding according to established investigative procedures."

He opened the pillbox carefully, revealing it to be completely empty. "And what, Canon Bott, do you normally keep in this pillbox?"

"Lozenges," Canon Bott replied quickly, his hands trembling slightly. "For soothing my throat after sermonising on Sundays. The congregation can be quite... demanding of one's vocal cords, you understand."

"Though," Dr. Bell observed with characteristic professional caution, "the pillbox is completely empty now. When did you last use these throat lozenges, Canon?"

This practical consideration seemed to increase Canon Bott's nervousness considerably, though Constable Fenchurch dutifully recorded the explanation in his notes whilst muttering about complications arising from logical analysis interfering with straightforward police work.

16

AS CLEAR AS MUD

T he formal interview process that followed proved even more challenging than evidence collection. Each guest was questioned systematically about their observations regarding Lord Oswald's behaviour throughout the evening, the circumstances surrounding port service, and any suspicious activities they might have noticed during dinner or its immediate aftermath.

Canon Bott's interview proved particularly fascinating.

"Canon," Constable Fenchurch began with official gravity, consulting his notebook for appropriate questioning procedures, "did you observe anything unusual about Lord Oswald's behaviour during the dinner conversation?"

"Unusual? Well, that is to say... he displayed rather antagonistic tendencies throughout the evening, one might observe. Quite reminiscent of the disagreeable character I've developed for chapter twelve of my current manuscript, though obviously real circumstances rarely mirror fictional constructions so precisely... though perhaps considering the dramatic irony of someone so thoroughly unpleasant meeting such a sensational end..." Canon Bott's nervous chatter gradually trailed off as he realised his response was providing considerably more information about his creative writing processes than the criminal investigation.

"Simply answer the question directly, Canon," Mrs. Tuggles interjected with motherly firmness that brooked no nonsense from overwrought clergymen. "Was Lord Oswald behaving strangely during dinner, or was he not?"

"He seemed entirely consistent with his established character," Canon Bott managed finally, his hands fidgeting with his manuscript pages in a manner that suggested protective anxiety about their contents. "Thoroughly disagreeable, certainly, but predictably so throughout the entire evening."

Captain Tuggles proved a considerably more straightforward witness, though his testimony became increasingly embellished with maritime analogies that seemed tangentially relevant at best to domestic poisoning investigations.

"The fellow was clearly sailing under false colours from the moment he set foot in this house," the Captain declared with naval authority, his bearing suggesting vast experience with assessing character under challenging circumstances. "Hostile intentions barely concealed beneath diplomatic protocol, rather reminiscent of certain Mediterranean privateers I encountered during classified operations involving international maritime security."

"Pirates?" Constable Fenchurch repeated, his confusion evident as he struggled to incorporate swashbuckling adventures into village murder investigations. "Were there actually pirates involved in Lord Oswald's death?"

"Metaphorical pirates, dear," Mrs. Tuggles clarified with patient understanding, clearly accustomed to translating her husband's colourful observations into practical meanings. "Captain Tuggles was drawing comparisons between Lord Oswald's general behaviour and various fictional maritime villains."

"Ah. I see. Though I'm not entirely certain how pirates, fictional or otherwise, relate specifically to deceased aristocrats, even metaphorically speaking."

Dr. Bell's testimony proved refreshingly factual and professional, focusing entirely on medical observations rather than creative interpretations of events that required additional explanation. Her clinical description of symptoms, precise timeline of developments, and expert assessment of probable causation provided exactly the sort of concrete information that murder investigations required for reaching reliable conclusions.

Fenchurch then turned his attention to Cecily.

17

LADY MURDERESS?

When Constable Fenchurch finally turned his attention to Cecily, his manner underwent a subtle but distinct transformation. Gone was the bumbling deference he'd shown whilst fumbling with his notebook and bicycle clips; instead, his expression assumed the gravity of someone finally arriving at the crux of his investigation. He consulted his notes with newfound confidence, clearly relishing what he perceived to be the most significant interview of his professional career.

"Lady Ashcombe," he began with official solemnity, his pencil poised with prosecutorial determination, "I must address certain uncomfortable facts that have emerged during this investigation. Facts that, I'm afraid, point rather directly toward your involvement in Lord Oswald's unfortunate demise."

Cecily felt her stomach drop whilst maintaining outward composure, though she noticed Dr. Bell's sharp glance of concern and Mrs. Fotheringill's barely perceptible stiffening from her position near the doorway.

"You see," Constable Fenchurch continued, warming to his theme with the enthusiasm of someone who'd discovered a satisfyingly straightforward solution to an otherwise bewildering case, "when one examines the evidence objectively, certain patterns emerge that cannot be ignored by responsible law enforcement, however personally distressing they might prove."

He flipped through his notebook with theatrical precision, clearly savoring the dramatic moment. "First, there is the matter of motive. Lord Oswald Crowthorne had legitimate legal claims to this very estate—claims that your unexpected inheritance directly contradicted. His continued existence posed a genuine threat to your newfound position as Lady of Ashcombe, did it not?"

"I was unaware of any competing claims," Cecily replied carefully, though she recognised the logic that would appear compelling to someone seeking convenient explanations for complex circumstances.

"Perhaps. Though one might reasonably observe that removing such inconvenient opposition would certainly benefit your interests considerably." Constable Fenchurch made elaborate notes whilst continuing his prosecution. "Second, we have the matter of opportunity. By your own admission, you personally served Lord Oswald the fatal beverage that resulted in his immediate death. Your hands touched his glass directly, providing perfect access for poison administration."

"At his specific request, as multiple witnesses have confirmed."

"Ah yes, his 'specific request,'" the Constable repeated with obvious skepticism, his tone suggesting considerable doubt about the convenience of this particular detail. "How remarkably fortunate that the victim himself provided such ideal circumstances for his own murder, wouldn't you agree?"

Dr. Bell's expression darkened dangerously at this implication, though she maintained professional silence whilst clearly struggling with considerable temptation to intervene on Cecily's behalf.

"Furthermore," Constable Fenchurch declared with mounting confidence, "one cannot ignore the remarkable coincidence that Little Codding has enjoyed decades of peaceful, law-abiding tranquillity—not a single serious crime in my entire tenure as village constable. Yet within mere weeks of your arrival from London, we suddenly find ourselves dealing with sophisticated murder involving exotic poisons and elaborate criminal conspiracies."

His voice carried the satisfaction of someone who believed he'd identified the obvious connection that explained everything troubling about recent events. "Prior to your residence at Ashcombe Hall, this community represented a perfect sanctuary of rural virtue and traditional English respectability. Now we have mysterious deaths, international intrigue, and criminal activities that belong in sensational novels rather than respectable village life."

The accusation hung in the air like smoke from a badly tended fire—acrid, offensive, and impossible to ignore despite everyone's desire for more pleasant circumstances.

"Are you suggesting," Cecily asked with dangerous calm, "that my mere presence somehow corrupted this community's moral character sufficiently to inspire murder among previously virtuous residents?"

"I'm suggesting," Constable Fenchurch replied with the stubborn certainty of someone who'd constructed a theory that satisfied his desire for simple answers, "that sophisticated criminal behaviour coinciding precisely with your arrival from metropolitan London suggests patterns that responsible investigators cannot reasonably dismiss as mere coincidence."

Captain Tuggles cleared his throat with the sort of maritime authority that preceded broadside artillery engagement. "Now see here, Constable, that's thoroughly inappropriate speculation about Lady Ashcombe's character based on nothing more than unfortunate timing."

"With respect, Captain, timing combined with motive, opportunity, and direct physical contact with the murder weapon presents compelling evidence that cannot be ignored simply because we all prefer more comfortable conclusions."

Mrs. Tuggles stepped forward with motherly indignation that suggested Constable Fenchurch was about to receive the sort of comprehensive moral education that had successfully reformed various unreasonable persons throughout her extensive experience with community management.

"Percy Fenchurch, you should be thoroughly ashamed of yourself for making such scandalous accusations against a lady who's shown nothing but kindness and propriety since arriving in our community. Your insinuations about London corruption and criminal influence are beneath contempt and entirely unworthy of your position."

Constable Fenchurch's confidence wavered slightly under this maternal assault, though he maintained his investigative position with visible determination to pursue what he clearly considered proper police work regardless of social pressure.

"I understand everyone's natural desire to defend Lady Ashcombe," he said with forced diplomatic patience, "but murder investigations require objective analysis of facts rather than personal sympathies, however understandable such loyalties might be."

"Then perhaps," Dr. Bell interjected with the crisp precision that had intimidated countless military personnel of superior rank, "you might explain how Lady Ashcombe managed to poison Lord Oswald's specific glass whilst serving identical port to everyone else at table, none of whom suffered any ill effects whatsoever?"

This practical consideration clearly hadn't occurred to Constable Fenchurch during his theoretical construction of Cecily's guilt, and his momentary confusion suggested that actual detective work required considerably more analytical complexity than he'd initially anticipated.

"Well... that is... obviously she employed some sophisticated method of selective poison delivery that... which would require additional investigation to determine precise technical details..." he stammered, his prosecutorial confidence deflating like a punctured bicycle tire.

"Obviously," Canon Bott murmured nervously, though whether he was supporting or questioning the Constable's reasoning remained diplomatically unclear.

The interview concluded with Constable Fenchurch's stern warnings about remaining available for further questioning, though his earlier certainty about Cecily's guilt had been considerably undermined by practical considerations that his theoretical case construction had failed to address adequately.

As he gathered his scattered notes and prepared for his dignified departure—which proved somewhat less impressive than intended due to persistent difficulties with his bicycle clips—the atmosphere in the drawing room settled into the sort of heavy tension that follows accusations too serious to ignore yet too poorly supported to inspire confidence in official investigative capabilities.

18

ELEGANT SIMPLICITY

By the time evening settled over Ashcombe Hall with autumn's characteristic early darkness, and the drawing room had acquired the peculiar oppressive atmosphere that inevitably accompanies locations where shocking events have recently disrupted normal social expectations. Shadows seemed longer, silence felt heavier, and every creak of the old house settling suggested mysterious activities rather than familiar domestic sounds.

Constable Fenchurch had departed with earnest promises to consult higher authorities about proper procedures for murder investigations that clearly exceeded village-level investigative capabilities, leaving behind official warnings that absolutely no one should even consider leaving Little Codding until the case achieved satisfactory resolution through appropriate legal channels.

"Well," Elsie observed once they were finally alone in the library, where a cheerful fire provided welcome contrast to the evening's grim developments, "that was thoroughly exhausting, and I'm not entirely confident that our well-meaning Constable possesses sufficient experience to solve complicated murder cases through conventional police methods."

Cecily settled wearily into the Earl's favourite wing-backed chair, her mind still reeling from the extraordinary transformation of what should have been a pleasant welcoming dinner into something resembling the sort of melodramatic mystery that Canon Bott apparently favoured for his literary efforts. Pip arranged himself across her feet with the solid warmth that suggested he understood emotional comfort was required, even if the specific circumstances exceeded normal canine comprehension.

"I keep thinking about Dr. Bell's observation," she murmured, staring into the dancing flames whilst her thoughts churned through the evening's bewildering sequence of events. "About how Oswald specifically requested that I pour his port personally, almost as though he anticipated some particular danger requiring special precautions."

"Or," Elsie suggested with characteristic directness, her expression grave with uncomfortable possibilities, "as though someone deliberately arranged circumstances to ensure you would be directly connected to whatever poison ultimately killed him."

Despite their mutual desire for simpler explanations that didn't involve deliberate criminal conspiracies targeting Cecily specifically, the thought that this perhaps was a conspiracy that went tragically wrong could not be ignored.

Perhaps Oswald conspired to implicate Cecily in an *attempted* murder? The more Cecily considered this possibility, the more disturbingly plausible it became. Oswald's insistence that she personally serve his port, his theatrical manner throughout the evening, even his pointed comments about inheritance claims—all could have been carefully orchestrated elements of an elaborate scheme designed to destroy her reputation and legal standing in the community.

"Think about it," Elsie said slowly, working through the implications aloud. "What if Oswald planned to consume a non-lethal dose of poison, something that would make him dramatically ill but not actually kill him? He could then claim you had attempted to murder him to secure your inheritance, with multiple witnesses having observed you personally serving the contaminated beverage."

Cecilys eyes widened with horrified understanding. "Such accusations would have been absolutely devastating, even if ultimately disproven. The scandal alone would have made my position here completely untenable."

"Precisely. And with his legal claims to the estate, however spurious, he could have pursued both criminal charges and civil litigation that would have tied up the inheritance indefinitely." Cecily felt a chill that had nothing to do with the autumn evening. "A brilliant scheme, really—except something went catastrophically wrong with the dosage."

The possibility that Oswald had accidentally poisoned himself while attempting to frame her for attempted murder was both ironically fitting and deeply unsettling. It suggested a level of malicious calculation that transformed him from merely disagreeable dinner guest to genuinely dangerous adversary, even in death.

"But that would also mean," Elsie said quietly, "that someone else knew about his plan and deliberately increased the poison to ensure fatal results. Someone who wanted Oswald dead and was perfectly willing to let you take the blame for it."

Elsie's tone carried the sort of grim certainty that came from systematic analysis of uncomfortable facts. "Consider the elegant simplicity—you inherited an estate he expected to receive, providing clear motive for wanting him eliminated. You poured the fatal drink with your own hands, establishing direct opportunity for poison administration. And his death permanently removes your primary legal challenger whilst simultaneously making you the most obvious suspect for criminal responsibility."

Cecily felt cold dread settling in her stomach as she contemplated the ruthless efficiency of this murderous strategy, assuming Elsie's assessment proved accurate.

"Which means," she said slowly, her voice barely above a whisper, "that someone planned Lord Oswald's death with considerable sophistication, using me as an unwitting accomplice whilst ensuring I would bear complete responsibility for the fatal consequences."

"Let us consider each guest methodically," Cecily decided, moving to the writing desk for paper and ink. "Means, motive, and opportunity for everyone present, examined as objectively as possible regardless of personal preferences."

Elsie settled beside her with the practical efficiency that had made her invaluable during times of tremendous pressure.

19

THE UNUSUAL SUSPECTS

"Dr. Bell first," Cecily began reluctantly, though examining her old friend's potential guilt felt like betraying fundamental trust. "She certainly possesses extensive medical knowledge regarding appropriate poisons and their effective administration methods."

"And she declared Lord Oswald dead rather quickly," Elsie added with obvious reluctance, clearly sharing Cecily's discomfort with suspecting someone they both respected. "Someone less charitable might suggest she was ensuring he couldn't recover regardless of whatever treatment possibilities might have existed."

"Though she also worked desperately to save him initially, and her rapid diagnosis protected everyone else from potential poisoning if the port supply had been generally contaminated." Cecily paused thoughtfully, balancing evidence that could support either innocence or guilt. "And although she clearly disliked the man, what conceivable motive could she have for wanting Oswald dead?"

"Unknown at present. Though she did mention previous wartime encounters with him, and her reaction suggested their shared history wasn't entirely pleasant or professional."

Cecily made careful notes about Dr. Bell's theoretical involvement whilst hoping desperately that continued investigation would eliminate rather than implicate her respected colleague in actual criminal activity.

"Canon Bott next. His nervousness throughout the evening exceeded anything reasonable for simply witnessing unexpected death, even violent death. And his pill box?"

"He was also protecting those manuscript pages rather defensively," Elsie recalled, her expression thoughtful. "Almost as though he feared someone might discover incriminating evidence amongst his creative writing efforts."

"His murder mystery research certainly provides access to information about killing methods, though that seems circumstantial evidence at best for actual criminal behaviour." Cecily considered the anxious clergyman's conduct throughout dinner and its aftermath. "Though I definitely noticed he seemed particularly uncomfortable whenever Lord Oswald made comments about family histories and buried village secrets."

"Possible motive involving something Oswald knew about Canon Bott's past activities or present circumstances that required permanent silence?"

"Perhaps. Though what secrets could a respectable village vicar possess that would justify murder to prevent exposure?"

They continued their systematic analysis through each dinner guest, carefully documenting potential motives, suspicious behaviour patterns, and opportunities for poison administration. The exercise proved both enlightening and deeply disturbing as uncomfortable patterns emerged suggesting that virtually everyone present had harboured some form of serious resentment or anxiety regarding Lord Oswald's presence and future intentions.

Captain and Mrs. Tuggles had appeared genuinely shocked by the sudden death, though their lengthy residence in Little Codding meant they possessed comprehensive knowledge about local history, family connections, and potential sources of conflict involving estate inheritance matters. If Oswald had somehow threatened established village relationships or individual security arrangements, their apparent respectability might effectively conceal fiercely protective instincts capable of extreme action.

The systematic review revealed profoundly uncomfortable truths about the complexity of human motivations and the genuine difficulty of distinguishing authentic grief from carefully performed innocence when everyone present possessed logical reasons for relief at Lord Oswald's permanent removal from their various community concerns.

"Most troubling of all," Cecily observed, completing her notes with growing unease about the implications of her analysis, "is how thoroughly this entire crime appears to have been planned specifically to implicate me. Someone studied tonight's social arrangements carefully enough to ensure the poison reached Oswald through my direct personal service whilst establishing my obvious guilt for any subsequent investigation."

"Which strongly suggests," Elsie replied grimly, her voice heavy with disturbing implications, "that whoever committed this murder knows you intimately enough to predict your likely behaviour and arrange circumstances accordingly."

Before Cecily could formulate an adequate response to this deeply unsettling consideration, Mrs. Fotheringill appeared in the library doorway, apparently undaunted by the late hour and extraordinary circumstances that had disrupted normal household routines.

"Lady Ashcombe," the housekeeper began with obvious reluctance to disturb private conversations, "I do hope

138

you'll forgive the intrusion, but I thought you should know that I've secured all remaining port wine and related glassware pending proper examination by qualified authorities."

"Thank you, Mrs. Fotheringill. That demonstrates excellent practical thinking under very trying circumstances."

As they discussed the troubling implications of their investigation, Cecily couldn't help but notice that Mrs. Fotheringill's hands appeared distinctly red and blistered, the skin looking raw and uncomfortable beneath the lamplight. The sight struck her as particularly unusual given the housekeeper's typically impeccable presentation and careful attention to personal grooming that befitted her professional position.

"Mrs. Fotheringill," Cecily said with genuine concern, recognising the sort of skin irritation that could prove both painful and persistently troublesome, "your hands appear quite inflamed. Are you quite all right?"

The housekeeper glanced down at her reddened palms with obvious embarrassment, clearly hoping the condition had escaped notice during her official duties. "Oh, that. Yes, well... I believe it must be the caustic soda in the washing suds, my lady. Though I confess it's rather peculiar that such irritation should develop now, having never troubled me before despite years of identical household procedures."

She flexed her fingers gingerly, wincing slightly at what was obviously considerable discomfort beneath her stoic professional demeanour. "Perhaps it's merely nervous tension, what with all the extraordinary circumstances we've endured this evening. The body does respond to shock in rather unexpected ways sometimes, doesn't it?"

The explanation seemed plausible enough, though Cecily filed the observation away with other potentially significant details that might prove relevant to understanding the complete sequence of events surrounding Lord Oswald's death. In her nursing experience, she'd learned that seemingly minor medical symptoms occasionally provided crucial insight into larger patterns requiring careful investigation.

"Additionally," the housekeeper continued, clearly struggling with internal conflict about proper discretion versus household loyalty, "I feel somewhat obligated to mention certain conversations I've overheard during recent weeks regarding Lord Oswald's visits to various village establishments and private residences."

Cecily's attention sharpened immediately at this unexpected intelligence. "What sorts of conversations, specifically?"

"Well, my lady, Lord Oswald had been making rather pointed inquiries about several local residents' personal histories and family circumstances. The sort of detailed questions that suggested he possessed uncomfortable knowledge about private matters that most people prefer to keep strictly confidential."

"Blackmail?" Elsie asked with characteristic directness, cutting straight to the heart of what Mrs. Fotheringill was diplomatically suggesting.

"I certainly wouldn't presume to make such serious accusations without substantial evidence," the housekeeper replied carefully, maintaining appropriate discretion whilst clearly conveying significant information. "Though I will say that more than one person has expressed genuine concerns about his apparent intentions regarding sensitive information that could prove socially or professionally devastating if revealed publicly."

This intelligence transformed their understanding of potential motives for Lord Oswald's murder completely. Rather than simple resentment about inheritance disputes or personal dislike of his disagreeable character, his death might have resulted from someone's desperate need to permanently silence dangerous threats to carefully guarded secrets.

"Do you know which specific individuals were particularly concerned about his inquiries into their private affairs?"

"I'm afraid that would constitute mere village gossip, my lady, and hardly appropriate for me to repeat without substantial verification of accuracy." Mrs. Fotheringill's expression suggested she possessed considerable additional information whilst maintaining appropriately professional standards about sharing unconfirmed intelligence that might damage innocent reputations.

"Of course. Though if you should remember anything definite that might help identify who genuinely wanted Lord Oswald permanently silenced, I do hope you'll share such information through appropriate channels."

"Indeed, my lady. Though I should perhaps mention that this household's reputation and your personal standing in the community now depend considerably upon resolving this matter satisfactorily, regardless of whatever unconventional investigation methods might prove necessary to achieve justice."

The housekeeper's carefully neutral tone conveyed an unmistakable message about expectations regarding Cecily's active personal involvement in clearing her name through whatever means the circumstances required, conventional or otherwise.

After Mrs. Fotheringill departed with her usual quiet efficiency, Cecily stared at her investigation notes whilst contemplating the overwhelming complexity of actual murder cases compared to the theoretical simplicity that Canon Bott's literary efforts apparently suggested for amateur detective work.

"'The heart is deceitful above all things, and desperately wicked: who can know it?'" she quoted softly, one of

Father's frequent reminders about human nature providing uncomfortable context for her current circumstances. "I trained as a nurse to heal people and preserve life, not to investigate their deliberate deaths or untangle webs of village secrets and criminal conspiracy."

"Then we'd better become exceptionally competent detectives with remarkable speed," Elsie replied with characteristic determination. "Because I strongly suspect Constable Fenchurch's well-meaning investigation will conclude with your arrest for murder unless we can provide him with considerably more compelling evidence pointing clearly toward the actual criminal."

Pip stirred restlessly against Cecily's feet, apparently sensing her emotional turmoil through whatever mysterious connection existed between devoted dogs and their troubled human companions.

Tomorrow, she would begin systematic investigation into Lord Oswald's death, employing whatever analytical skills her wartime nursing experience had provided for dealing with complex problems in overwhelming circumstances.

Tonight, she could only pray earnestly that truth would ultimately prove more compelling than circumstantial evidence, and that divine justice would prevail over convenient conclusions that satisfied surface appearances whilst ignoring deeper realities about actual guilt and innocence.

Though given her increasingly precarious legal position, she rather suspected that ensuring proper justice would require considerably more active personal participation than simply trusting others to discover truth through conventional investigation methods.

The grandfather clock in the entrance hall chimed midnight, marking the end of what had begun as a hopeful celebration of her new life at Ashcombe Hall and had concluded with her transformation from grateful inheritor to suspected murderess requiring urgent vindication through amateur detective work she'd never imagined herself capable of conducting.

She could only hope that morning would indeed bring clarity, truth, and the sort of divine assistance that her current circumstances seemed to desperately require.

20

A HATBOX OF SECRETS

Dawn crept across the Rose Room's mullioned windows with the hesitant grey light of late October, carrying the sort of melancholy that seemed to seep into one's very bones. Cecily woke to the uncomfortable sensation of emerging from troubling dreams, only to discover that reality had acquired distinctly nightmarish qualities requiring immediate attention.

The previous evening's events arranged themselves in her memory with unwelcome clarity—Lord Oswald's theatrical collapse, Dr. Bell's grim diagnosis, and deeply troubling recognition that she occupied the position of primary suspect in a murder carefully orchestrated to implicate her specifically.

Tea arrived with Mary's usual gentle efficiency, though the young maid's expression carried new undertones of worry that suggested the household staff were painfully aware of their mistress's precarious situation.

"Morning papers, my lady," Mary said quietly, setting down the silver service whilst clearly struggling with anxiety. "Though perhaps... there's been considerable discussion in the village regarding last evening's events."

Cecily accepted the carefully folded newspaper with mounting dread, suspecting that village journalism would favour dramatic speculation over careful analysis of actual facts.

The headline exceeded even her pessimistic expectations: "MYSTERIOUS DEATH AT ASHCOMBE HALL: Local Aristocrat Dies Under Suspicious Circumstances."

"Well," she murmured to Pip, who had positioned himself across the bed's foot with characteristic determination to provide moral support, "I suppose sensational reporting was inevitable."

Pip responded with sympathetic tail wagging that suggested complete confidence in her innocence regardless of whatever theories the outside world might develop.

Elsie arrived bearing additional tea and wearing the expression of someone who had been conducting early morning intelligence-gathering.

"The situation is precisely as grim as we anticipated," she announced without preliminary pleasantries. "Half the village believes you've committed murder for financial gain, whilst the other half considers you too obviously guilty to have actually done it."

"I'm not entirely certain whether that constitutes improvement," Cecily observed dryly, setting aside the newspaper with distaste.

"Mrs. Fotheringill mentioned something rather interesting," Elsie continued, settling into the window seat. "Young Timothy from the post office observed Lord Oswald visiting Marjorie Blight's shop twice this past week, engaged in what he described as 'heated discussions' involving considerable... animation."

This intelligence immediately captured Cecily's attention, perhaps Margaret held secrets she was not lettig on.

"What manner of discussions?"

"Timothy's eavesdropping proved inadequate for details, though he noted that Marjorie appeared distinctly distressed following each visit, closing her establishment early both days."

Cecily considered this whilst recalling her conversation with Marjorie during yesterday's village introductions. The milliner had displayed remarkable knowledge about Lord Oswald's inheritance expectations, accompanied by pointed warnings about "stirring up old troubles."

"Perhaps we should examine Miss Blight's establishment more thoroughly than social visits typically permit,"

Cecily decided, her wartime experience providing useful precedents for necessary investigations despite conventional constraints.

"Excellent reasoning. Though we'll require a strategic approach—something allowing proper examination without arousing suspicion about our detective activities."

The solution possessed elegant simplicity: hat shopping. Perfectly reasonable behaviour for Lady Ashcombe, establishing her wardrobe according to elevated social requirements.

An hour later, they approached the millinery shop with carefully rehearsed enthusiasm for acquiring fashionable headwear. The morning had developed into one of those crisp autumn days when sunshine struggled through increasingly determined clouds, whilst the village bustled with activity suggesting most residents were attempting to restore familiar routines.

Despite the hour when normal business should have commenced, Marjorie's shop remained shuttered, with drawn curtains preventing interior observation.

Cecily knocked firmly, producing an authoritative sound that conveyed expectation of immediate attention.

Several minutes passed before footsteps approached, accompanied by multiple locks being disengaged with obvious reluctance.

Marjorie appeared wearing defensive anxiety poorly concealed beneath professional courtesy. Her usually elaborate presentation had been reduced to practical simplicity, sharp eyes darting nervously between them and the street beyond.

"Lady Ashcombe," she said with forced brightness that failed to mask tension. "How... delightful. Though I'm afraid the shop isn't quite... I'm conducting inventory this morning..."

"We've come specifically hoping to discuss hat requirements for my new social position," Cecily interrupted gently but firmly. "I find myself woefully unprepared for entertaining and community involvement."

Mentioning commercial prospects proved precisely correct for gaining admission despite Marjorie's obvious reluctance.

"Of course! How thoughtless... naturally a lady in your position requires... please, do come in," Marjorie stammered, professional enthusiasm gradually overcoming personal anxiety.

The shop's interior appeared considerably dishevelled compared to yesterday's careful arrangements. Hat boxes lay scattered across surfaces, various materials suggesting hasty searching rather than systematic inventory.

"I apologise for the... disarray," Marjorie said, beginning rapid attempts to restore order. "Extensive reorganisation of stock..."

Under cover of Elsie's theatrical hat examination—complete with rapturous commentary about peacock feathers and artificial orchids—Cecily began casual migration toward the shop's rear section, where private business materials were presumably stored.

"Marjorie," she called with studied casualness, "might I examine your mourning collection? Formal requirements will continue, yet I shouldn't appear entirely unfashionable."

"Certainly! The mourning pieces are in the back room—please browse freely," Marjorie replied, relief evident about directing attention away from her searching activities.

The back room revealed organised chaos speaking of urgent investigation without concern for normal procedures. Papers lay scattered, drawers hung open, personal items distributed beyond original boundaries.

Cecily began systematic examination under pretence of reviewing hat options whilst maintaining awareness of conversation from the main shop, where Elsie continued elaborate fashion commentary requiring extended consideration.

Her investigation quickly revealed items of potential significance. A small money box lay open, contents scattered, revealing receipts for transactions that appeared unusually frequent for a village millinery establishment.

The receipts bore dates spanning several years, documenting regular payments described simply as "monthly considerations" in modest but consistent amounts. Several bore Lord Oswald's initials alongside brief notations indicating "L.B. matters" and "as discussed."

Most intriguingly, photographs were tucked between papers—images depicting a young child at various ages, accompanied by a woman who might have been Marjorie's sister, given certain familial resemblances in features.

Additional photographs proved curious rather than immediately revealing. Several showed the same child with a young man whose stance seemed remarkably like that of Miles Penrose, whilst another figure appeared partially visible in the background of one image. Cecily recognised the gait of Dr. Bell, though the photograph's age made identification uncertain.

Before she could examine these materials thoroughly, Pip announced his presence through characteristic investigation of interesting scents leading to a wooden box beneath a work table. His determined excavation efforts eventually dislodged the container, sending contents spilling across the floor.

"Pip, cease immediately!" Cecily whispered urgently whilst diving to gather evidence before Marjorie discovered their activities.

The newly revealed documents proved intriguing without being immediately conclusive. Medical receipts from a local practice documented "pediatric consultations" spanning multiple years, with payment arrangements that seemed unusually complex for routine care.

Most concerning was a recent note bearing Lord Oswald's handwriting, dated one week previous, containing language about "reviewing current arrangements due to changing circumstances" and "reconsidering ongoing commitments."

The letter's tone suggested tension rather than mere administrative adjustment, though its precise implications remained unclear without additional context.

Behind the receipts and photographs, Cecily's mood was lightened when she discovered a small bookshelf housing a collection of Silas Bellweather mystery novels. Several volumes bore the telltale signs of devoted readership— spines cracked from frequent handling and pages softened by countless turnings. One particular tome, 'The Gentleman's Deadly Secret,' appeared especially cherished, its cover worn smooth by admirers' fingers.

Cecily suppressed a smile of amusement as she contemplated whether Marjorie remained blissfully unaware that her beloved literary hero was none other than their own nervous rector. The delicious irony that Canon Bott's clandestine authorial pursuits had found such enthusiastic appreciation within the very village he served struck her as precisely the sort of revelation that would send him into one of his characteristic states of anxious palpitations.

"Perhaps I might read one myself, a little light amusement might help me sleep," she thought, just as Marjorie's voice indicated imminent conclusion of inventory activities.

"Lady Ashcombe? Have you found anything suitable? I do hope my organisational efforts haven't disrupted proper browsing."

"Nothing quite appropriate yet," Cecily replied with forced casualness whilst hastily replacing documents and extracting herself with reluctant Pip. "Perhaps we might continue selection another day? I require additional consideration about appropriate styles."

This diplomatic postponement clearly relieved Marjorie, whose anxiety had mounted visibly despite commercial interest in substantial purchases.

Their departure involved elaborate promises about future visits and purchasing once circumstances achieved resolution. Marjorie's farewell carried obvious relief.

Only upon their emergence from the shop did anyone notice that Pip had acquired a particularly fetching cloche hat adorned with jet-black feathers, which he wore with the dignified air of one who understood that proper attire was essential when conducting serious detective work. The hat sat at a jaunty angle between his ears, secured by what appeared to be a delicate ribbon that had somehow become entangled during his enthusiastic investigation of the millinery's lower regions, and he showed no inclination whatsoever to surrender this fashionable acquisition despite Cecily's mortified attempts at retrieval.

"Fascinating visit," Elsie observed once beyond observation. "Your expression suggests considerably more success than mine with millinery. What did you discover?"

Cecily provided comprehensive summary of financial records, photographs, and correspondence establishing Lord Oswald's involvement in complex arrangements requiring secrecy and substantial expense over multiple years.

"Some kind of financial arrangement with Oswald, and medical services?" Elsie questioned. "Perhaps discontinued support would provide an excellent murder motive."

"Precisely. Though I remain uncertain why such elaborate concealment was necessary." Cecily paused, troubled by implications about people she'd begun trusting. "Most disturbing is the possibility of Miles Penrose and Dr. Bell's involvement."

The possibility that her respected colleague might be implicated provided deeply unsettling context for the previous evening's events.

21

THE MYSTERIOUS MR. BELLWEATHER

Mrs. Fotheringill greeted their return with obvious relief that her mistress had completed village business without additional complications.

Duchess, meanwhile, with a wary eye, swept past them in the hallway like a silver-backed judge—glanced up, bestowed one imperious stare, then vanished down the grand staircase as if to announce, 'I approve this detour to town.'

"How did your shopping proceed, my lady?"

"Quite enlightening, though we've postponed purchases pending resolution of current complexities," Cecily replied carefully.

"Understandable. Though Constable Fenchurch called during your absence, requesting additional questioning of household staff. I scheduled his visit for tomorrow morning."

This confirmed increasing urgency of discovering actual evidence before official inquiries resulted in formal charges.

Evening found them in the library, reviewing investigation notes whilst attempting to develop coherent theories about criminal responsibility that would provide alternatives to obvious guilt suggested by circumstantial evidence.

"Perhaps we should examine the Earl's library more thoroughly," Elsie suggested. "If Lord Oswald maintained previous familiarity through family connections, there might be records providing context."

Amongst the Earl's organised materials, they discovered family photographs spanning generations of social activities and community involvement.

One image immediately captured attention. The photograph depicted Lord Oswald as a younger man with several companions whose bearing suggested visiting London friends participating in country entertainment. The group posed with local young ladies whose dress identified them as village residents during mixed social occasions bringing together gentry and families before the war transformed traditional relationships.

Most intriguingly, one lady bore an unmistakable resemblance to a younger and more rotund Marjorie Blight, another to a youthful and unconventionally pretty Dr. Ball, though the photograph's age made definitive identification challenging despite striking similarities.

Whilst examining another section of the Earl's collection, Cecily spotted a copy of 'The Gentleman's Deadly Secret' by Silas Bellweather nestled between volumes of botanical studies and agricultural reports. The incongruous placement amused her considerably, given the Earl's reputation for scholarly pursuits rather than sensational fiction.

"Perhaps a touch of literary escapism might provide relief from our current all too real criminal mysteries," she murmured, curious to see how Canon Bott's alter ego measured against his pulpit personality. Pulling the volume from the shelf, she was surprised to see that the book looked as if it had been handled recently. There were smudges on some of the pages—faint traces of rouge or lipstick—and a subtle, lingering scent of juniper clinging to the pages.

Setting the book aside for later, she turned her attention to matters far more urgent—and, regrettably, not the stuff of fiction.

They continued examining documents until well past respectable hours, producing substantial evidence about complex relationships whilst clarity about criminal responsibility remained frustratingly elusive.

Outside, autumn wind moved restlessly through bare branches, creating shifting shadows across diamond-paned windows. Pip's presence, and her dear friend Elsie, offered assurance that she needn't face challenges entirely alone.

"'If any of you lack wisdom, let him ask of God, that giveth to all *men* liberally,'" Cecily admonished herself.

She could only hope providence would provide whatever evidence and wisdom circumstances required for ensuring justice prevailed over expedient solutions.

Though given the mounting complexity they'd already discovered, reaching the truth would require considerably more detective work than time might ultimately permit.

∿

Later that night, Cecily found herself unable to sleep, the weight of discoveries and implications swirling around her mind like an Autumn storm.

Making her way back to the library, Cecily found herself drawn to the Earl's pristine copy of 'The Gentleman's Deadly Secret.' The irony that she should seek refuge in fictional murder whilst embroiled in all too real criminal circumstances was not lost upon her, though perhaps Canon Bott's literary escapades might provide precisely the mental respite required after such an exhausting day of investigation.

She settled into the Earl's favourite wing-back chair beside the library's dying fire, Pip arranging himself across her feet with characteristic determination to provide comfort during troubled times. The cloche hat he'd liberated from Marjorie's establishment had been diplomatically removed and set aside for future return, though his dignified expression suggested he considered the accessory rightfully acquired through legitimate detective work.

"Well, Pip," she murmured, opening the volume to its first chapter, "let us discover whether our nervous vicar possesses greater talent for fictional murders than we've witnessed in solving actual criminal activities."

The novel's opening immediately captured her attention through elegant prose describing a country house mystery bearing remarkable similarities to their current circumstances. Canon Bott—or rather, Silas Bellweather —had crafted a tale involving aristocratic inheritance, family secrets, and suspicious deaths that seemed almost prescient given recent events.

As she progressed through the narrative, Cecily found herself genuinely impressed by the quality of characterisation and plotting. The mysterious Mr. Bellweather demonstrated considerable skill in developing complex relationships between characters whilst maintaining the sort of genteel atmosphere that made murder seem almost civilised rather than sordid.

The fictional detective proved particularly engaging—a competent young sleuth relying on unconventional methods. This literary hero possessed medical training, sharp observational skills, and the sort of practical intelligence that enabled effective investigation despite social obstacles.

"How curious," Cecily observed softly, noting additional parallels between fictional and actual events. "One might almost suspect Canon Bott of possessing prophetic abilities regarding criminal complications."

The plot's development revealed elaborate schemes involving forged documents, concealed identities, and financial arrangements designed to protect family honour whilst concealing scandalous truths. It was all very intriguing.

As the evening advanced and shadows deepened across the library's familiar surroundings, Cecily found herself completely absorbed in the narrative's intricate plotting. Canon Bott's literary talents far exceeded anything she might have anticipated from their nervous rector, whose public presentations suggested considerably less competence than his fictional creations demonstrated.

The story's hero employed investigative methods that struck Cecily as remarkably practical, including systematic examination of suspects' private papers and careful analysis of financial arrangements. These fictional techniques provided useful inspiration for approaching her own criminal complexities with greater methodology.

Chapter by chapter, she progressed through the tale whilst the fire gradually reduced to glowing embers and the house settled into its familiar nocturnal quietude. The novel's atmosphere of genteel mystery seemed perfectly suited to her current circumstances, offering both entertainment and unconscious instruction regarding detective procedures.

Pip maintained his position across her feet, occasionally shifting to accommodate more comfortable arrangements whilst providing steady warmth that anchored her to peaceful domesticity despite literary adventures in fictional criminality.

As two o'clock approached, marked by the grandfather clock's bronze chimes echoing through silent corridors, she discovered herself reluctant to abandon the story despite growing drowsiness. The novel's concluding chapters promised dramatic revelations that would expose the murderer's identity through systematic elimination of false theories.

Her eyes grew increasingly heavy as warmth from the dying fire combined with Pip's comforting presence to create irresistible somnolence. The book's pages seemed to blur slightly as her attention wavered between fictional detection and the growing appeal of restful unconsciousness.

"'He that keepeth thee will not slumber,'" she whispered drowsily. Whatever tomorrow might bring with Constable Fenchurch's questioning, providence would provide the necessary wisdom for navigating challenges with integrity intact.

The novel slipped gradually from her relaxing grasp as sleep claimed her consciousness, leaving Silas Bellweather's fictional mystery unresolved whilst real criminal complications awaited resolution through her own investigative efforts. In dreams, literary and actual mysteries blended together, creating scenarios where Canon Bott revealed murderers with theatrical flourishes whilst Pip discovered crucial evidence hidden in millinery establishments.

The library's peaceful atmosphere embraced her slumber with familiar comfort, book resting against her lap whilst firelight faded to darkness and the house maintained its protective watch over troubled dreams that mixed fictional detection with all too real concerns about justice, truth, and the preservation of honour amidst criminal accusations that threatened everything she held dear.

22

GRAVES AND REVELATIONS

The morning brought unwelcome but necessary visitors in the form of Constable Fenchurch and what appeared to be his entire collection of official notebooks, evidence bags, and a magnifying glass that suggested he'd been consulting detective manuals with renewed determination overnight. His bicycle clips remained stubbornly attached despite having dismounted some time ago, creating the impression of someone prepared for hasty retreat should circumstances demand it.

"Lady Ashcombe," he announced with forced authority whilst juggling his investigative materials, "I require additional questioning of household staff regarding Wednesday evening's... regrettable events."

Cecily received him in the morning room, where Mrs. Fotheringill white gloved hands had arranged tea with

164

characteristic efficiency despite obviously strained circumstances. The housekeeper's expression suggested she possessed very firm opinions about policemen who disrupted proper household routines whilst failing to demonstrate adequate competence.

"Naturally, Constable. Though I do hope you'll conduct interviews with appropriate consideration for staff sensibilities. Murder investigations can prove rather overwhelming for people unaccustomed to criminal complications."

"Quite so. Though I must mention that preliminary inquiries have revealed certain... irregularities requiring clarification."

His uncomfortable manner suggested these irregularities pointed directly toward her guilt rather than alternative explanations.

"What specific irregularities, if I may ask?"

Constable Fenchurch consulted his notebook with obvious importance. "Well, Lord Oswald's London solicitor has expressed considerable surprise about his client's sudden death, particularly given recent correspondence indicating renewed interest in challenging the estate inheritance through legal channels."

This struck Cecily with unpleasant implications about timing and potential motives for eliminating opposition through permanent means.

"I see. Though surely Lord Oswald's inheritance expectations were known to many people beyond myself? His disappointments weren't precisely secret."

"Perhaps not. Though few people possessed such obvious financial motivation for ensuring his permanent silence." The Constable's tone carried increasing confidence about her probable guilt. "Additionally, village inquiries have revealed that you visited Miss Marjorie Blight's establishment yesterday morning, shortly before she mysteriously closed her shop and departed for unspecified personal business."

Cecily felt alarm settling in her stomach as she realised their investigation had attracted official attention.

"Hat shopping hardly constitutes suspicious behaviour, Constable. Ladies of my position require appropriate accessories for social obligations."

"Naturally. Though several witnesses observed Miss Blight's obvious distress following your visit."

Before Cecily could formulate an appropriate response, Pip announced his presence by discovering Constable Fenchurch's evidence bag and launching an enthusiastic investigation of its fascinating contents.

The resulting chaos involved scattered official documents, a thoroughly slobbered magnifying glass, and Pip's triumphant discovery of wrapped sandwich remnants that clearly required immediate consumption despite questionable provenance.

"That animal," Constable Fenchurch observed with mounting exasperation whilst attempting to restore order, "demonstrates remarkable talent for disrupting official police procedures."

"Pip merely maintains active curiosity about his surroundings," Cecily replied diplomatically whilst extracting her dog from continued evidence tampering. "Though perhaps we might confine him during formal interviews to prevent additional... complications."

Following Constable Fenchurch's departure— accompanied by earnest warnings about remaining available for further questioning—Cecily and Elsie gathered at the library windows to observe his unsteady bicycle progress down the drive.

"He's definitely developing theories about your guilt," Elsie observed grimly. "And Marjorie's convenient disappearance provides additional circumstantial evidence suggesting conspiracy."

"Which means we require actual evidence proving alternative theories before his investigation concludes with my arrest," Cecily replied, her nursing training providing useful experience with urgent deadlines. "Mrs. Fotheringill mentioned that Jeremiah Crimp had observed unusual nighttime activities around the estate grounds recently. Perhaps we should investigate more thoroughly."

The village churchyard occupied ancient ground where generations of Little Codding residents had found final rest amongst weathered headstones and carefully tended graves. Autumn had advanced sufficiently that most trees stood bare against grey sky, their branches creating delicate tracery suggesting ecclesiastical architecture designed by divine rather than human inspiration.

Jeremiah Crimp proved easy to locate through the melodious whistling of hymns that echoed amongst the tombstones. His work rhythm possessed the steady competence of someone who'd spent decades maintaining sacred ground whilst contemplating mortality's lessons. Jeremiah was the proud digger of every hole in Little Codding since 1881.

He was a man of perhaps sixty years whose face bore the weathered dignity of extensive outdoor labour. His bearing conveyed quiet wisdom that developed through years of listening to confessions whispered over fresh graves.

"Good morning, Mr. Crimp," Cecily called, approaching with respect for both his person and the sacred nature of his workplace. "I wondered if we might discuss certain observations you've made regarding unusual activities near Ashcombe Hall recently."

Jeremiah paused his digging to regard them with keen intelligence that suggested considerably more awareness than his humble occupation might typically encompass.

"Aye, Lady Ashcombe. Been expecting someone would come asking about the night wanderers eventually," he replied, his voice carrying the soft Oxfordshire accent of generations rooted in local soil. "Though I'll admit surprise it's yourself rather than official authority conducting such inquiries."

"Constable Fenchurch appears... occupied with other investigative priorities," Cecily said diplomatically. "Though I remain quite concerned about estate security."

"Quite proper, considering circumstances." Jeremiah leaned against his spade whilst his thoughtful gaze assessed their characters and motivations. "Though I suspect ye already know these weren't casual poachers seeking convenient game birds."

"What manner of people, then?"

"Folks with specific business requiring darkness for concealment, it seems."

Jeremiah shifted uncomfortably, his weathered hands working at the brim of his cap as though it might provide some escape from Cecily's expectant gaze. The gravedigger, who had spent decades keeping the village's secrets buried alongside its dead, appeared to be wrestling with his conscience.

"Well, my lady," he began, his voice carrying the reluctant tone of a man forced to speak when silence would serve him better, "I don't make it my business to go about telling tales, you understand. A man in my profession learns to keep his counsel."

"Of course, Mr. Crimp," Cecily replied gently, sensing that whatever revelation lay ahead required careful handling. "But if what you saw might help us understand what happened to Lord Oswald..."

Jeremiah's weathered face creased into deeper lines. "Aye, well... the thing is, I was working late that evening, tidying up after the Widow Stirk's mother-in-law's interment. Proper fuss she made about the flowers, that one did. Anyway, I was making my way home when I caught sight of movement near the folly." He paused, clearly struggling with the propriety of his next words. "Saw someone skulking about, I did. Thought it might be young lads up to mischief, but..."

"But?" Elsie prompted, unable to contain her curiosity.

"It were Mr. Penrose, miss. Your chauffeur. And he weren't alone." Jeremiah's voice dropped to barely above a whisper. "Had a young lady with him, he did. Pretty thing, couldn't have been more than twenty, if that. And before you ask, my lady, they weren't discussing the weather, if you catch my meaning. Saw them in what you might call... an embrace."

Cecily felt her cheeks warm slightly. The revelation of Miles's romantic entanglements was hardly scandalous by modern standards, yet something about Jeremiah's obvious discomfort suggested there was more to the story.

Before she could respond, Pip chose that moment to demonstrate his characteristic disregard for serious conversation. The terrier, who had been investigating something fascinating near a moss-covered headstone, suddenly took off at full speed towards the older section of the graveyard, his excited barks echoing off the ancient stones.

"Pip! Come back here this instant!" Cecily called, but her command fell upon selectively deaf ears.

The three of them set off in pursuit, weaving between weathered monuments and carefully tended plots. Pip, clearly revelling in this impromptu game of chase, had disappeared behind a particularly elaborate Victorian memorial dedicated to someone's "Beloved Wife and Mother, Gone to Glory."

"Blasted dog," Elsie muttered, gathering her skirts as she navigated around a crumbling stone cherub. "Why must he always choose the most inconvenient moments to—"

Her complaint was cut short by a spectacular crash as she collided with an abandoned wheelbarrow that had been left beside a freshly dug plot. Arms windmilling frantically, Elsie toppled backwards into the contraption, her legs kicking helplessly in the air whilst her hat tumbled into a nearby patch of primroses.

"Oh, my word!" Cecily rushed to assist, though she had to bite her lip to suppress an entirely inappropriate giggle at the sight of her maid's black-stockinged legs protruding from the wheelbarrow like some peculiar garden ornament.

Jeremiah, displaying surprising agility for his years, helped extract Elsie from her predicament. "Right as rain, miss," he assured her as she brushed dirt from her uniform with wounded dignity. "Happens to the best of us. That wheelbarrow's caught more ankles than a tangled fishing net."

"Well, I never," Elsie huffed, retrieving her hat and jamming it rather forcefully back onto her head. "What sort of person leaves gardening equipment lying about a graveyard?"

Their question was answered by a series of vigorous scraping sounds emanating from behind the memorial. Following the noise, they discovered Pip engaged in what could only be described as his life's work—digging. Earth flew with remarkable efficiency as the terrier excavated what appeared to be a significant crater beside a pair of modest headstones.

"Good heavens," Jeremiah observed with genuine admiration, "that little fellow's got proper form, he has.

Look at that technique—paws working in perfect rhythm, nice deep cuts. I've seen grown men manage less impressive excavation work."

Cecily approached the graves, reading the inscriptions with growing interest. The first headstone, though weathered, bore clear lettering: "Thomas Penrose, Beloved Husband and Brother, Died in Action 1918, Greater Love Hath No Man." Beside it lay another stone: "Sarah Penrose Blight, Beloved Wife of Ten Years, Died 1919, 'Until We Meet Again.'"

"Penrose," Cecily murmured thoughtfully. "Related to Miles, I wonder?"

Jeremiah nodded slowly. "Aye, that'd be his elder brother, Tom. And his wife, Sarah. Proper sad tale, that one. Caused quite the stir in the village back then, it did."

"What sort of stir?" Cecily asked, though she suspected she already knew the answer.

The gravedigger glanced around as though the very headstones might gossip, then leaned closer. "Well, my lady, Sarah was... shall we say, in a delicate condition when she and Tom married. This were back in 1907 or thereabouts, my memory fails me, and the wedding came about rather suddenly, if you catch my meaning. Course, Tom swore up and down the child was his, but tongues will wag, especially when a pretty girl finds herself in such circumstances."

"People questioned the child's parentage?" Elsie asked, her eyes bright with the sort of intrigue that made village scandals irresistible.

"Oh, they did more than question it, miss. Some right cruel things were said. Drove the young couple clear out of Little Codding, they did. Moved up to Yorkshire, where Tom could find work and they could start fresh. Then the war came, and Tom enlisted straightaway. Killed at Passchendaele, poor lad. Body never came home, but Sarah insisted he be remembered here, where his family was buried."

Jeremiah's voice grew softer. "Sarah followed him the next year. Some said it was the Spanish flu, others claimed it was a broken heart. But there were whispers... well, there's always whispers when a young woman dies sudden-like. Suicide, like. Her sister, Majorie, requested she be buried here, beside where Tom's memorial stands."

"And the child?" Cecily asked gently.

"Little Lucy. Sweet thing, she was. Hair like spun gold and the brightest blue eyes you ever did see. But Codding hasn't seen her since they left. And after Sarah passed..." Jeremiah trailed off, looking uncomfortable once again.

At that moment, Pip emerged from his excavation project, proudly carrying something in his mouth. Upon closer inspection, Cecily realised it was a small bouquet of flowers—daffodils and early roses, tied with a faded blue ribbon. Attached to the stems was a piece of paper that had somehow survived the dog's enthusiastic retrieval.

Cecily carefully extracted the note from Pip's jaws, unfolding it to reveal childish handwriting in pencil: "Forever missed."

The three humans stared at the note in silence. Finally, Jeremiah spoke, his voice barely audible. "Well, I'll be blessed. Someone's been tending to Sarah's grave all these years."

A fat raindrop splashed onto the note in Cecily's hand, followed quickly by another. The sky, which had been threatening all afternoon, finally made good on its promise. Within moments, the gentle patter became a proper downpour.

"Run for it!" Elsie called, and the unlikely quartet— woman, maid, gravedigger, and muddy terrier—made a dash for the shelter of Ashcombe Hall.

As they reached the edge of the graveyard, Cecily couldn't shake the feeling that they were being observed. Glancing back through the curtain of rain, she caught a glimpse of movement among the trees that bordered the far side of the cemetery. Just a shadow, perhaps, or someone taking shelter from the sudden storm.

But as they hurried towards the warmth and safety of the Hall, that shadow seemed to follow their progress with uncomfortable intensity before melting back into the darkness of the woods.

The mysteries of Little Codding, it seemed, were multiplying rather faster than Cecily had anticipated.

23

TEA AND TRAPS

As they entered the Hall's welcoming warmth, Mrs. Fotheringill materialised with her customary efficiency, though her expression carried undertones suggesting household concerns beyond normal domestic management. Her keys jangled softly at her waist as she moved to accept their outdoor garments. Cecily was also pleased to note that her hands were now completely healthy, having recovered from whatever malady had afflicted them over the past days.

"Lady Ashcombe, several messages arrived during your absence," the housekeeper announced whilst coordinating their coats with practised precision. "Canon Bott requests private audience regarding matters of considerable importance. Additionally, Lady Fenella sent word claiming to possess important information requiring immediate discussion."

"Lady Fenella?" Cecily repeated with genuine surprise, raising an eyebrow at this unexpected development.

The Dowager Lady Fenella Crowthorne—her predecessor's gloriously scandalous sister—had graciously decided to remain in residence at the Hall's east wing following the Earl's passing, an arrangement she'd described as her "magnanimous concession to domestic harmony."

The woman who attributed her remarkable vitality to gin's preserving properties and considered a slice of lemon in her evening cocktail the pinnacle of healthy eating had thus far maintained diplomatic distance from recent tragic events, preferring to observe household drama from behind her collection of crystal glasses.

Lady Fenella had long ago disowned any connection with her nephew Oswald, declaring him a tedious bore who possessed all the charm of stale toast and twice the arrogance. Indeed, she'd once confided that had she been younger and more agile, she might have considered drowning him herself in a bath of gin and tonic—though she'd hastily added that wasting perfectly good gin on such an enterprise would constitute the greater crime.

"The Dowager Lady claims to have experienced... spiritual revelations regarding Wednesday evening's tragedy," Mrs. Fotheringill replied with diplomatic neutrality that carefully concealed personal opinions about supernatural communication methods. "Her exact words involved 'ethereal messages from the departed' and 'urgent demands for justice from beyond the veil.'"

Cecily nodded with mild amusement, having heard of Lady Fenella's modern fascination with Conan Doyle and his outlandish imaginings. Her father warned her of such things, and felt thankful for her more stalwart spiritual roots.

"And finally, my lady," Mrs. Fotheringill continued whilst maintaining her carefully neutral expression, "Dr. Bell has requested a private audience and has been waiting for your return in the morning room, claiming to possess information of relevance. She said it was a matter of urgency."

Cecily exchanged meaningful glances with Elsie.

"Please arrange meetings with Canon Bott and Lady Fenella for later this afternoon," Cecily decided, her wartime experience having taught her that information must be pursued methodically despite competing demands for attention. "I shall speak with Dr. Bell immediately."

Mrs. Fotheringill nodded approvingly at this decisive approach, though her expression suggested continued reservations about the wisdom of entertaining so many potentially unreliable witnesses within a single day.

Cecily's found Dr. Bell in the morning room, occupying the wing chair beside the fire with characteristic composure that failed to entirely conceal underlying agitation. Her usually impeccable appearance showed subtle signs of distress—hands clasped rather too tightly, medical bag positioned defensively across her knees as though prepared for immediate departure.

"Winifred, how good of you to wait," Cecily began, settling across from her colleague with studied casualness designed to encourage confidential disclosure. "Mrs. Fotheringill mentioned you wished to discuss matters of relevance."

Dr. Bell's response emerged with obvious reluctance, suggesting internal struggle between professional discretion and personal conscience that was producing considerable mental conflict.

"Cecily, I fear I may have... inadvertently contributed to yesterday evening's tragedy through professional consultation provided months previous," she said, her characteristic confidence replaced by uncharacteristic uncertainty. "Something most unusual occurred here in Little Codding that now appears disturbingly significant."

She paused, gathering courage for revelations that clearly caused considerable distress despite their necessity under current circumstances.

"Canon Bott visited my surgery approximately thirty-six months before his official appointment to the parish, seeking what he termed 'academic consultation' regarding alkaloid poisoning for purposes he claimed were purely theoretical in nature."

This intelligence immediately captured Cecily's complete attention, particularly given their mounting suspicions about the rector's nervous behaviour and mysterious literary pursuits.

"He enquired specifically about methods for administering lethal doses whilst minimising detection possibilities," Dr. Bell continued with growing horror at implications she was beginning to recognise. "The consultation seemed peculiar for clerical purposes, yet his ecclesiastical position suggested legitimate academic interest rather than criminal planning."

Cecily felt her stomach contract with growing dread whilst maintaining outward composure necessary for encouraging complete disclosure of whatever intelligence Dr. Bell possessed.

"Being a man of the cloth, presuming scholarly research, I shared comprehensive information about how one might achieve fatal results through careful calculation of dosage relative to body weight, optimal delivery methods for rapid absorption, and timing considerations for avoiding immediate detection during social circumstances."

Dr. Bell's voice carried mounting anguish as the full implications of her unwitting contribution became clear through recent events requiring expert knowledge for successful execution.

"I fear, Cecily, that my professional expertise may have inadvertently equipped a murderer with precisely the technical knowledge necessary for last evening's crime," she concluded miserably. "Though I make no direct accusations, the coincidence appears too remarkable for comfortable dismissal."

***

The afternoon brought precisely the sort of domestic chaos that transforms a civilised drawing room into a theatrical battlefield. Canon Bott arrived first, announced by Mrs. Fotheringill with the expression of someone presenting evidence of general moral decline in modern society. He entered the morning room with his characteristic nervous energy, clutching a leather portfolio and wearing the haunted look of a man whose literary secrets might be exposed at any moment.

"Lady Ashcombe," he began, settling into a chair with obvious reluctance, "I must confess that recent events have created considerable... that is to say, the circumstances surrounding Lord Oswald's demise have produced certain... complications regarding my position in the community."

Canon Bott's nervous energy intensified perceptibly as he began his account, his leather portfolio clutched against his chest like protective armour. His voice adopted the hesitant cadence of a man attempting to navigate treacherous conversational territory whilst maintaining some semblance of clerical dignity.

"Lady Ashcombe, I find myself compelled to share intelligence that may prove... illuminating regarding recent tragic circumstances," he began, his words emerging in carefully measured phrases designed to minimise personal liability whilst maximising dramatic impact. "Several years past, I made certain academic enquiries of Dr. Bell regarding matters of... shall we say, theoretical pharmaceutical interest."

He paused, allowing this revelation to achieve its intended effect before continuing with growing confidence that suggested relief at finally unburdening himself of uncomfortable knowledge.

"During our consultation, I discovered that Dr. Bell possessed remarkably comprehensive understanding of alkaloid administration—not merely theoretical knowledge, you understand, but practical expertise regarding dosage calculations, delivery methods, and timing considerations for avoiding detection during social circumstances."

His voice carried mounting excitement as he warmed to his theme, the nervous rector transforming into something approaching an investigative enthusiast despite his obvious distress at the implications.

"Her knowledge extended far beyond what one might expect from standard medical training," he continued, leaning forward conspiratorially. "She demonstrated intimate familiarity with precisely the sort of technical details that would prove essential for... for achieving the tragic results we witnessed Wednesday evening."

Canon Bott's expression grew increasingly troubled as he approached the most delicate portion of his revelation, his clerical sensibilities clearly warring with his desire to present compelling evidence of suspicious circumstances.

"However reluctant I remain to suggest that a respected medical professional might involve herself in criminal activities, I feel duty-bound to inform you that village gossip has long suggested certain... irregular associations between Dr. Bell and the late Lord Oswald."

He lowered his voice to confidential tones that barely concealed his obvious fascination with the scandalous nature of his intelligence, despite the moral disapproval such fascination ought to inspire in a man of his calling.

"Mrs. Tuggles mentioned observing clandestine meetings between them in times past—encounters that appeared neither professional nor entirely... respectable in nature. The good Captain's widow possesses sharp eyes for detecting improper conduct, and her observations suggested associations that extended well beyond normal doctor-patient relationships."

Canon Bott's delivery achieved crescendo as he reached the most explosive element of his disclosure, his nervous energy finally finding outlet through dramatic revelation that would have impressed theatrical audiences despite its potentially devastating implications for village respectability.

"Furthermore," he whispered with the air of a man sharing state secrets, "persistent rumours suggest these irregular meetings may have produced... consequences of the sort that create permanent complications for all parties concerned. There has been considerable speculation regarding a child—an illegitimate offspring whose existence would certainly explain both the secretive nature of their continued association and the potential for murderous desperation should exposure threaten professional reputation."

The canon's complexion achieved unhealthy pallor as the full implications of his accusations settled upon his ecclesiastical conscience, which clearly recognised the gravity of suggesting that a respected physician might commit murder to conceal scandalous personal history.

"I make no direct accusations, you understand," he concluded hastily, his earlier confidence evaporating as moral uncertainty reasserted itself. "Yet the combination of technical expertise, personal motivation, and opportunity appears too remarkable for comfortable dismissal by responsible investigators seeking truth regarding Wednesday's tragedy."

His portfolio trembled slightly in his hands as he awaited Cecily's response to these revelations that transformed

Dr. Bell from respected colleague into potential murderess driven by secrets that could destroy both professional standing and personal reputation should they achieve public exposure.

Before Cecily could respond to this stammering confession, the doors burst open with histrionic force that would have impressed the West End's finest dramatic productions. Lady Fenella swept into the room like a magnificent battleship entering harbour, resplendent in emerald silk adorned with enough jewellery to stock a modest establishment in Bond Street. Her silver hair was arranged in elaborate waves that defied both gravity and contemporary fashion, whilst her rouge had been applied with the generous hand of someone who considered subtlety a character flaw in lesser mortals.

"Darling Cecily!" she proclaimed, arms extended as though embracing the entire universe, "I bring revelations from beyond the veil! The departed have spoken, and their messages demand immediate attention!"

Canon Bott's reaction to this pronouncement suggested he'd been struck by divine lightning whilst simultaneously discovering his worst theological nightmares manifesting in reality. His portfolio tumbled to the carpet, scattering papers like autumn leaves in a stiff breeze.

"Lady Fenella," he managed weakly, "such... such declarations regarding communication with the... the deceased... surely you cannot seriously suggest..."

"Cannot suggest what, my dear canon?" Fenella inquired with saccharine sweetness that carried distinct undertones of impending warfare. "That the spirits possess wisdom beyond our mortal comprehension? That those who have passed beyond earthly concerns might observe truths hidden from our limited perception?"

She settled into the largest chair with the air of a monarch claiming her rightful throne, producing a crystal tumbler from her reticule. The vessel appeared to contain gin with a decorative slice of lemon that she claimed constituted adequate nourishment for maintaining her remarkable vitality.

"The invisible realm, canon, operates according to principles that transcend your narrow ecclesiastical training," she continued, taking a generous sip whilst fixing him with eyes that sparkled with malicious amusement. "Last evening, during my customary consultation with the ethereal plane, dear departed Harold—my second husband, you understand—provided most illuminating intelligence regarding Wednesday's tragedy."

Canon Bott's theological sensibilities appeared to be experiencing complete collapse under this assault upon orthodox doctrine. "Lady Fenella, the Church's position on... on such matters is quite clear... communication with the dead is expressly... that is to say, Deuteronomy specifically prohibits..."

"Poppycock!" Fenella interrupted cheerfully. "Harold was never one for biblical restrictions whilst living, and death has certainly not improved his respect for canonical authority. He informed me quite distinctly that gentlemen often conceal deadly secrets behind facades of respectability."

"Secrets?" Canon Bott squeaked, his voice achieving registers normally associated with choir boys experiencing unfortunate changes in vocal development.

"Indeed, my nervous friend. Harold was most emphatic about the treacherous nature of masculine deception. He ought to know, having maintained three separate households during our marriage—though I only discovered the third after his funeral, when an exotic dancer from Brighton arrived claiming widowhood."

Cecily found herself caught between horrified fascination and barely suppressed amusement as these two opposing forces of village society engaged in theological combat. Canon Bott represented orthodox respectability, whilst Fenella embodied everything that made conventional morality collapse into nervous hysteria.

"Lady Fenella, surely you cannot expect rational people to accept that your deceased husband provides criminal intelligence through... through supernatural consultation," Canon Bott protested, though his conviction appeared to weaken under her magnificently shameless assault.

"Why not, dear canon? Your profession claims considerably more outrageous supernatural communications, yet you present them as established fact rather than personal revelation. At least my spirits offer practical advice about murder rather than abstract moralising about redemption."

Canon Bott's mouth opened and closed silently whilst his brain attempted to formulate responses that would defend orthodox doctrine without offending a woman whose eccentricity was matched only by her complete indifference to conventional opinion.

"The Bible... that is... divine revelation operates through established channels... properly ordained ministry..." he managed eventually, though his arguments seemed to dissolve under Fenella's amused contempt.

Fenella took another appreciative sip whilst regarding him with the expression of a cat contemplating a particularly plump mouse. "Tell me, canon, do your established channels provide any intelligence about recent criminal activities? Or do they confine themselves to abstract platitudes about loving one's neighbours?"

The poor rector's expression suggested his established channels were currently providing no assistance whatsoever with managing this particular crisis of faith and social diplomacy.

"The Church's sacramental system... proper liturgical framework... centuries of theological development..." he attempted, though his defence seemed to crumble with each word.

"Oh, liturgical framework," Fenella mused dismissively. "Harold mentioned something about liturgical frameworks during last evening's consultation. He said gentlemen often hide behind impressive terminology whilst conducting thoroughly disreputable activities. Rather like writing sensational fiction whilst pretending to be respectable clergy, one might suppose."

Canon Bott's complexion achieved the sort of pallor normally associated with marble statuary as this observation struck uncomfortably close to his most carefully guarded secrets.

"I'm sure I don't understand what you might suggest..." he whispered, though his guilty expression indicated perfect comprehension of exactly what was being suggested.

"Of course not, dear man. Gentlemen never understand when their secrets are perfectly transparent."

Cecily decided intervention might prevent actual, not merely theological warfare from erupting in her morning room. "Lady Fenella, perhaps your spiritual consultations revealed specific intelligence about Wednesday evening's events?"

She had no intention of entertaining Fenella's imaginings, but deference to age demanded that the dowager be allowed to air her views.

"Most certainly, darling," Fenella agreed, though her eyes remained fixed upon the still-scrambling canon with predatory satisfaction. "Harold was most insistent that gentlemen who maintain secret lives become increasingly dangerous when circumstances threaten exposure."

"Secret lives?" Stuttered Canon Bott.

"Of course, dear Canon," Lady Fenella said with theatrical flair, "the spirits have mentioned rather specific concerns about concealed literary endeavours containing uncomfortable resemblances to actual criminal activities recently perpetrated against innocent victims."

This supernatural intelligence struck Canon Bott with obvious terror, his complexion shifting through various alarming shades suggesting serious cardiovascular distress requiring immediate medical attention.

"Literary endeavours?" he repeated faintly, clutching his portfolio with renewed desperation whilst perspiration beaded upon his forehead. "Surely fictional creative writing cannot possibly... that is, mere coincidental similarities between artistic imagination and unfortunate real circumstances hardly constitute evidence of criminal involvement or premeditated conspiracy!"

"Lady Fenella," Cecily ventured with diplomatic precision whilst maintaining the delicate balance between respectful curiosity and gentle scepticism, "I cannot help but wonder whether these remarkable revelations might have originated from earthly sources rather than ethereal consultations. Perhaps your spiritual intelligence was acquired through reading certain... contemporary fictional works that perhaps bear coincidental resemblances to our current circumstances?"

The dowager's emerald silk rustled with indignant energy as she drew herself to magnificent height, crystal tumbler raised like a battle standard against such sacrilegious doubt. Her jewellery clinked with righteous fury as she gestured expansively, dismissing such pedestrian explanations with magnificent disdain that brooked no argument from mortals who failed to appreciate supernatural methodology.

"The invisible realm, darling Cecily, does not require assistance from sensational publications to communicate urgent intelligence!"

Lady Fenella concluded her magnificent defence with characteristic flair, sweeping toward the doors with the dramatic force of a West End finale. Her emerald silk trailed behind her like royal robes as she paused for one final pronouncement that would leave lasting impression upon her startled audience.

"Harold was never wrong about detecting masculine duplicity during forty-three years of marriage, my dear, he was an expert!" she declared, "I shall retire to my chambers for further consultations, though I suspect the departed have already provided sufficient intelligence."

With that magnificent exit, she swept from the room.

Canon Bott remained frozen in his chair for several moments after her departure, perspiration beading upon his forehead as implications of her accusations settled upon his increasingly agitated conscience. When he finally spoke, his voice carried the tremulous quality of a man whose carefully constructed facades were crumbling.

"Lady Ashcombe, I fear I must take my leave before... that is to say, current circumstances require immediate attention to pressing ecclesiastical obligations," he stammered. "However, I feel duty-bound to emphasise that my previous knowledge regarding Dr. Bell's technical expertise and questionable associations with the deceased remains worthy of serious consideration from responsible investigators."

"Furthermore," he continued, warming to this theme that directed attention away from his own compromising circumstances, "I have observed that your chauffeur, Mr. Penrose, may be someone you want to consult. Though he is a quiet man, his entanglements may surprise you"

With this elusive parting accusation, Canon Bott clutched his portfolio and departed with obvious relief.

24

MILES OF MYSTERY

The motor car bay stood open to the afternoon air, and within its shadowed depths, Miles Penrose was bent over the bonnet of a vintage Bentley like a surgeon over his patient. Oil-stained coveralls hung loose on his lean frame, and his sleeves were rolled back to reveal forearms corded with muscle and marked by the careful attention of someone who understood machinery better than most men understood themselves.

Cecily approached with Elsie trailing behind, their footsteps crunching on the gravel. Miles didn't look up immediately—merely continued his methodical work, adjusting something deep within the engine's bowels with the concentration of a priest at prayer.

"Good afternoon, Miles," Cecily ventured, her voice

carrying that particular tone she reserved for conversations she suspected might prove difficult.

He straightened slowly, wiping his hands on a rag that had seen better decades. His grey eyes met hers with the directness of a man who'd learned that dancing around subjects was a luxury few could afford. "Lady Cecily." A nod to Elsie. "Miss Pickering."

"Lovely old motor," Cecily observed, running her fingers along the Bentley's polished wing. "Getting her running again?"

"Engine's sound enough," Miles replied, his voice carrying the measured cadence of someone who chose his words as carefully as he selected his tools. "Just needs proper attention. Most things do."

Elsie shifted beside her, and Cecily could practically feel her maid's impatience radiating like heat from a forge. But Miles Penrose wasn't a man to be hurried, and rushing him would be rather like trying to push the tide— pointless and likely to leave one thoroughly soaked.

"Miles," Cecily began, settling herself on a wooden crate that served as makeshift seating, "I wonder if we might have a word about your evening walks."

His hands stilled on the engine, though his expression remained carefully neutral. "Not against the law, last I checked."

"No indeed. Though one might wonder what draws a man to the old folly at such peculiar hours." She kept her tone light, conversational, but watched his face carefully. "Rather a romantic spot, wouldn't you say?"

Something flickered in Miles's eyes—not guilt, precisely, but the wariness of a man who'd spent too many years keeping secrets to give them up easily. He resumed his work, but his movements had lost their earlier fluidity.

"Might be someone finds comfort there," he said finally. "Quiet places. Good for thinking."

"Or for meeting someone," Elsie interjected, earning herself a sharp look from both Cecily and Miles.

"Elsie," Cecily murmured, then turned back to Miles with renewed gentleness. "I'm not here to pry into your personal affairs, truly. But with everything that's happened—Oswald's death, all the questions swirling about—I find myself rather concerned for everyone's safety. Including yours."

Miles set down his spanner and straightened, fixing her with a look that seemed to weigh her words against some internal measure. When he spoke, his voice carried a roughness that hadn't been there before.

"My brother Edward married a young lady," he said abruptly. "Sarah Blight, her name was. Sweetest thing you ever saw, with eyes blue as summer sky and a laugh that could charm birds from trees."

Cecily blinked at the unexpected turn, but remained silent, sensing that interrupting now would be rather like stopping a rusty engine mid-turn—it might not start again.

"Edward loved her with everything he had," Miles continued, his gaze distant. "But Little Codding's a small pond, and when Sarah quickened with child barely six months after the wedding..." He shrugged, the gesture heavy with old pain. "Well, gossip spreads faster than oil on water, and twice as messy."

"People can be terribly unkind," Cecily said softly.

"Aye. Whispers followed them everywhere—timing's all wrong, they said. Baby came too early, or the wedding came too late." His jaw tightened. "Edward tried to shield her from it all, but Sarah heard every word. Cut her deep, it did. Drove them from the village, babe in arms."

Miles returned to his work, but his hands moved with less certainty now, as though the telling had unsettled his usual mechanical precision. "Then the war came calling, and Edward answered. Sarah was left alone with their young girl."

"He didn't return," Cecily said gently. It wasn't a question.

"Shrapnel took him at Passchendaele, and we remembered him right here in Little Codding graveyard." Miles's voice had dropped to barely above a whisper. "Sarah held on for a time, but a broken heart and the shame of it all… it ate at her like rust through steel. They found her in the river one morning, peaceful as you please. She'd always said she wanted to be buried next to the man she loved, and the best we could do was place her beside my brother's memorial."

Elsie's sharp intake of breath broke the heavy silence. Cecily felt her heart constrict with sympathy for the tragedy of it all.

"The child?" she asked.

"Little Lucy. My niece" Miles's expression softened fractionally. "Been like a daughter to me ever since. Marjorie Blight—Sarah's sister—and I, well, we've done what we could over the years. Sent her away to school, kept her safe from the worst of it. Seems Majorie had more to do with her directly over the years than I did, and financial arrangements with Oswald, but I don't know the details. Miss Blight always insisted family matters should remain secret, especially sensitive ones."

"And now Lucy's returned," Cecily said, understanding beginning to dawn.

Miles nodded slowly. "Been here in the village for quite some time. Grown into a fine young woman, she has. Wanted to come home, tend her parents' graves proper-like. Can't say I blame her, but..." He gestured helplessly. "She's using another name—Thompson—doesn't want to stir up the old scandal again. Bad enough she had to grow up with it hanging over her head."

"So your meetings in the graveyard—"

"She's family," Miles said firmly. "Only family I've got left, truth be told. Been meeting her quiet-like, helping her without drawing attention. Girl's been through enough."

The protective edge in his voice was unmistakable, and Cecily felt a rush of respect for this quiet man who'd spent years shielding a child from the malicious whispers of others. It painted his taciturn nature in an entirely different light—not unfriendliness, but the careful reserve of someone who'd learned to guard what mattered most.

"Oswald," she said carefully, "did he know about Lucy's return?"

Miles's hands clenched into fists, oil-stained knuckles standing out like accusation marks. "That pompous peacock knew everything and nothing, if you take my meaning. Heard whispers, caught wind of old scandal, but never bothered learning the truth of it."

"What did he threaten?"

"Said he'd make sure everyone knew Tom's daughter was back, carrying her shame like a banner. Promised he'd see she was driven out again, along with anyone fool enough to help her." Miles's grey eyes had gone hard as flint. "Talked about cleaning up the village, removing undesirable elements."

"You must have been furious," Elsie said.

Miles turned that steady gaze on her. "Reckon I was. Even if his stories are true, the only father that girl ever knew was my brother. But there's a difference between wanting a man gone and actually putting him in the ground, Miss Pickering. Army taught me to kill when necessary, but it also taught me discipline."

The words hung in the air between them, neither confession nor denial, but something more complex. Cecily found herself believing him, though whether that spoke to his honesty or her own preferences, she couldn't say.

"Where is Lucy staying?" Cecily asked.

"Small cottage on the far side of the village. Keeps to herself mostly, but she's a good girl. Deserves better than what this place gave her family."

Cecily stood, brushing dust from her skirts. The pieces of Miles's story fitted together with the neat precision of well-machined parts, each element supporting the whole. It explained his protectiveness, his careful nature, even his choice to remain largely solitary—a man safeguarding secrets had little room for casual friendships.

"Thank you for telling us," she said. "It can't have been easy."

Miles shrugged, already turning back to his engine. "Lady Cecily, your father was a decent man, and you've been decent to all of us here. Seemed right you should know the truth of it, rather than letting gossip fill in the blanks."

"Will you tell Lucy I'd like to meet her? When she's ready, of course."

"I'll ask her," Miles said after a pause. "But the decision's hers to make. Girl's entitled to her privacy, after everything."

As they walked back toward the house, Elsie fell into step beside Cecily, her expression thoughtful. "Do you believe him?"

"I think," Cecily said slowly, "that Miles Penrose is exactly what he appears to be—a decent man trying to protect his family from a world that's shown them precious little kindness."

"And Oswald's threats?"

"Were real enough, I'd wager. The question is whether they were sufficient motive for murder, or simply another example of his talent for making enemies." Cecily paused at the garden gate, watching Miles's figure bent once again over the Bentley's engine. "Though I suspect we've only heard part of the story."

"Always more layers to peel back," Elsie agreed. "Rather like an onion."

"Yes," Cecily murmured, "and just as likely to bring tears before we're finished."

25

MISS THOMPSON'S TROUBLE

M iss Thompson's cottage proved a small but meticulously maintained dwelling whose modest garden suggested pride in personal independence despite limited resources. Smoke curled from the chimney, whilst carefully mended curtains spoke of domestic competence maintaining comfortable circumstances through determined effort.

The young woman who answered their knock confirmed family resemblance to Marjorie whilst displaying gentler features suggesting sweeter temperament. Lucy appeared perhaps sixteen years old, with intelligent dark eyes that carried wariness suggesting she carried silent burdens.

"Ma'am," she said with obvious respect, though her attention moved nervously between Cecily and Elsie with uncertainty about unexpected visitors.

"Hello, Lucy, I'm Lady Ashcombe from the Hall, and Miss Pickering. We'd like to discuss certain family matters that might prove important for resolving recent difficulties."

Lucy's complexion paled significantly whilst her hands trembled as she invited them inside with reluctant courtesy.

The cottage's interior reflected careful housekeeping and creative resourcefulness that transformed limited space into genuinely comfortable accommodation. Everything appeared spotlessly clean, whilst small decorative touches spoke of artistic sensibilities developing beauty from modest materials.

"Miss Thompson," Cecily began carefully, recognising the girl's obvious anxiety, "I understand you may have been receiving financial assistance from Lord Oswald Crowthorne over the years, possibly through arrangements involving your aunt Marjorie."

Lucy's brows furrowed as she glanced between her visitors, confusion written all over her face.

"I don't know anything about Lord Oswald or any arrangements," she said quite frankly.

"Lucy," Elsie interjected gently, her paternal tone encouraging honesty, "circumstances have developed beyond simple family privacy. Lady Ashcombe faces serious accusations that might be resolved through truth rather than continued concealment protecting people who never deserved such loyalty."

"I'm afraid I know nothing about Lord Oswald," she said finally. "Aunt Majorie never mentioned him. Though I've heard that folks in the village consider him a frightfully nasty character."

"Lord Oswald died during dinner on Wednesday evening. Dr. Bell believes he was poisoned."

The shock on Lucy's face was obvious.

"I'm sorry for speaking ill of the dead," she managed to stutter, "but I know nothing of Lord Oswald's arrangements. Perhaps Aunt Marjorie might be able to help?"

∿

Bidding farewell to Lucy Thompson, Cecily and Elsie traversed the narrow lane leading away from the modest cottage, their footsteps echoing against the moss-covered stone walls that bordered the path. The girl's evident bewilderment regarding Lord Oswald's arrangements had left them with more questions than answers, though her genuine shock upon learning of his demise suggested complete ignorance of any family connection.

"Well, that proved enlightening," Elsie remarked, adjusting her hat against the afternoon breeze. "Though not quite in the manner we anticipated."

Cecily nodded thoughtfully, her mind wrestling with the contradictions emerging from their investigation. "Either Lucy Thompson possesses extraordinary theatrical abilities, or she truly knows nothing about receiving financial support from our deceased lord, if indeed there was any. Her confusion appeared entirely authentic."

"Which rather puts paid to any theory about parentage and payments, doesn't it?" Elsie observed, stepping carefully around a particularly deep puddle. "If Lucy knows nothing about Lord Oswald's arrangements, then what of the receipts we found?"

The puzzle pieces refused to arrange themselves into any coherent pattern. Cecily found herself considering each suspect with growing frustration, recognising that opportunity and motive seemed abundantly distributed amongst their dinner guests, and some of her chief suspects were not even present at the dinner. The solution seemed frustratingly elusive.

"Consider our cast of suspects," she mused aloud. "Canon Bott possessed clear motive if Lord Oswald threatened his literary aspirations somehow, or perhaps the Canon has a dark past even murkier than his novels. Mrs. Fotheringill faced potential dismissal, and certainly had means and opportunity. Miles harbours understandable disdain for Oswald, although being so emotionally opaque, it's hard to say what troubles him so deeply, plus he was not even present at the dinner. Dr. Bell, as much as it pains me to say so, is possibly the only person with clear know-how to dispatch someone so expertly through chemical means. Even Nancy Crimp suffered professional rejection."

"Don't forget Marjorie," Elsie added. "Though like Miles, she was not even present so it's hard to include her in the list of genuine suspects."

They paused at the village crossroads, where weathered signposts pointed toward various destinations with cheerful optimism that belied the complexity of their current situation. Cecily studied the painted directions thoughtfully, recognising that their investigation had reached similar crossroads.

"The most maddening aspect," she continued, "involves the practical difficulties surrounding the actual poisoning. How did anyone manage to administer poison specifically to Lord Oswald's port without affecting other guests? The bottle was opened at the table and consumed by all present."

Elsie frowned, clearly wrestling with the same challenge. "Unless someone managed to tamper with his particular glass beforehand, though goodness knows how they could guarantee he'd receive that specific vessel."

The sound of approaching huffing drew their attention, and they observed Percy Fenchurch riding toward them on his somewhat elderly bicycle, his constable's helmet slightly askew and his expression bearing its customary mixture of earnest determination and barely concealed panic.

"Lady Ashcombe!" he called, dismounting with more enthusiasm than grace. "I've been searching everywhere for you. Most urgent developments."

Cecily and Elsie exchanged glances, recognising that Percy's notion of urgent developments often proved somewhat relative.

"What seems to be the matter, Constable?" Cecily enquired politely.

Percy removed his helmet and wiped his brow with considerable ceremony. "Well, my lady, I've been conducting what you might call thorough investigations into this poisoning business, and I've discovered some rather disconcerting evidence."

"Indeed? What manner of evidence?"

"Actually, a complete lack of it. The port, the bottle, the tumbler..." He paused for dramatic effect. "None of them showed any trace of poison."

Elsie raised an eyebrow. "You mean the port was not the avenue of intoxication?"

Percy's expression grew somewhat uncomfortable. "Well, you see, my lady, that's precisely the conundrum. The laboratory chap in the county town was quite definitive—no trace of poison whatsoever in the port decanter or Lord Oswald's glass. Not a whiff of anything untoward."

Cecily felt her stomach lurch slightly. "I beg your pardon?"

"Clean as a whistle, both of them," Percy continued, removing his helmet to scratch his head in obvious bewilderment. "Yet Doctor Smith of Upper Codding examined the body again this morning at my request, and he's adamant that Oswald's death was most certainly not natural. All the signs point to poisoning, he says, but we haven't the foggiest idea how the poison was administered."

Elsie's eyebrows shot up. "You mean someone managed to poison Lord Oswald without actually poisoning him?"

"Precisely!" Percy exclaimed, though his triumph at stating the problem clearly did nothing to mask his complete bafflement at solving it. "The question is how, and I'm afraid I'm rather at a loss. If not the port, then what? And how did they manage it without affecting anyone else at dinner?"

Cecily felt the investigation taking yet another bewildering turn. "This certainly complicates matters considerably. We'd been operating under the assumption that the port was the delivery method."

"Indeed, and now I'm back at square one," Percy admitted, his confidence visibly deflating. "Both Dr. Bell and Dr. Smith insist the symptoms were consistent with some form of toxic substance, but if it wasn't in his drink..." He trailed off helplessly.

"Perhaps we should return to the Hall and examine everything more thoroughly," she suggested diplomatically. "There must be something we've overlooked."

Percy brightened considerably. "Excellent suggestion, my lady. Though I confess I'm rather stumped about where to look next."

As they walked toward the village centre, Cecily continued pondering the expanding web of suspects and motives. Each conversation revealed new complexities whilst failing to eliminate any potential culprits. The realisation that multiple individuals possessed reason to harm Lord Oswald created a particularly vexing situation —and now the method itself remained completely mysterious.

"The difficulty," she confided quietly to Elsie, "lies not in discovering who might have wished Lord Oswald harm, but rather in determining who possessed both the means and the nerve to act upon such wishes. And now we don't even know what those means were."

"Quite right," Elsie agreed. "And we're still no closer to understanding how the poison was actually administered. Until we solve that puzzle, all the motives in England won't convict anyone."

The village shops came into view, their cheerful facades maintaining determined optimism despite the shadow cast by recent events. Marjorie Blight's establishment stood prominently amongst them, its window display featuring an array of elaborate millinery creations that suggested both artistic ambition and perhaps questionable taste.

Cecily found herself hoping that a return to the scene of the crime might finally provide the breakthrough their investigation desperately needed, whilst simultaneously recognising that Percy's revelation had thrown any current theories into complete disarray.

26

THREE O'CLOCK IN THE MORNING

The grandfather clock's mournful chimes marked three o'clock in the morning, finding Cecily still tossing restlessly amongst her pillows whilst sleep proved as elusive as the identity of Lord Oswald's murderer. Pip quietly snored doggie snores at the end of the bed. The events of the past days circled through her thoughts with maddening persistence—the dinner party's tragic conclusion, the bewildering array of suspects each harbouring secrets that might justify homicide, and the frustrating absence of any clear method by which poison could have reached its intended victim.

Finally abandoning all pretence of slumber, she reached for the oil lamp beside her bed and settled back against the headboard with Silas Bellweather's novel. The volume bore the distinctive musty scent that marked all products of Pemberton & Associates' printing establishment along with the hint of juniper she'd sensed when she first pulled the book from its shelf in the Earl's library. Perhaps reading might lull her finally to sleep.

The novel had thus far proved typically sensational, featuring the mysterious death of a particularly disagreeable gentleman during an elaborate house party. The similarities to her own circumstances were undeniably disturbing, though Cecily found herself admiring the methodical approach Bellweather's detective employed whilst pursuing his investigation.

She had reached the final chapter now, titled 'A Brimful of Secrets', where the assembled suspects awaited revelation of the murderer's identity. Detective Inspector Mortimer gathered the house party guests in the library, his manner suggesting complete confidence in the solution he was about to present.

"Ladies and gentlemen," Mortimer announced with theatrical flourish, "you have all wondered how poison could have reached Colonel Blackwood's brandy when the bottle was opened at table before witnesses, poured immediately, and consumed without delay. The answer, I'm afraid, proves devastatingly simple."

Cecily found herself leaning forward with genuine interest, recognising the parallel to her own puzzling circumstances.

"The poison," Mortimer continued, "was never in the brandy at all. Our murderer employed a far more cunning method..."

Cecily's breath caught as the fictional revelation unfolded.

Setting the book aside with trembling fingers, her mind raced as the implications crystallised with startling clarity. The method described was not merely fictional cleverness —it explained everything about Lord Oswald's death that had previously seemed impossible.

The investigation that had seemed hopelessly complex suddenly appeared far more manageable, as did the motive.

As dawn approached, Cecily felt the peculiar satisfaction of a puzzle finally yielding to persistent examination. The fictional Detective Inspector Mortimer had inadvertently provided the key to solving a very real murder—and now she need only to reveal the truth.

The grandfather clock chimed four times as she finally extinguished her lamp, her mind at last sufficiently settled to permit rest.

Tomorrow would bring fresh opportunities to test her theory, and perhaps finally unmask the clever murderer who had turned Lord Oswald's own vanity into the vehicle of his destruction.

27

THE GRAND REVEAL

The drawing room at Ashcombe Hall had been restored to its former elegance, though the Persian rug bore faint testimony to Wednesday evening's tragedy. Afternoon light slanted through diamond-paned windows, casting long shadows that seemed to whisper of secrets finally ready to emerge from darkness into truth.

Mrs. Fotheringill had arranged the seating with tactical precision that would have impressed military strategists, ensuring optimal observation angles whilst maintaining social proprieties despite extraordinary circumstances.

Pip had appointed himself guardian of proceedings, positioning strategically beneath Cecily's chair with alert vigilance.

Duchess, too, swept into the room and vaulted gracefully onto the mantelpiece above the fireplace, fixing Pip with a cool, unblinking stare. Pip paused, clearly weighing his options, and settled back—truce declared. Today, there were bigger battles at play.

"Ladies and gentlemen," Cecily began, "we meet to unravel Lord Oswald Crowthorne's death. Truth, not assumption, will guide us."

"Ladies and gentlemen," Cecily began, drawing upon her wartime experience addressing medical staff during crisis situations, "we gather to address the tragic circumstances surrounding Lord Oswald Crowthorne's death. Justice demands complete understanding rather than convenient assumptions."

Constable Fenchurch occupied his chair near the doorway with visible importance that barely concealed his bewilderment. His notebook lay open with determined preparation to document proceedings accurately, though his expression suggested uncertainty about managing voluntary murder confessions during afternoon tea.

The assembled company created a tableau of barely concealed tensions and secrets. Canon Bott shifted uncomfortably in his chair, clutching his manuscript portfolio as though seeking spiritual protection against complicity in criminal activities, whilst nervous perspiration betrayed his continuing anxiety despite the afternoon's coolness.

Across from him, Dr. Bell struck a pose of clinical composure that reflected her medical training, though observant eyes might notice how her hands trembled slightly—a telling reminder of the lethal information her privileged position as a physician afforded her. Skills that could quickly dispatch an aristocrat with no trace, it appeared.

Lady Fenella had transformed her chair into something resembling a theatrical throne, her peacock feathers and elaborate jewellery catching the light with each dramatic gesture. Her sharp eyes darted between speakers whilst she radiated supreme confidence that her ethereal interjections had provided the crucial assistance required to deliver swift and awful justice.

The Tuggleses presented a stark contrast to the surrounding nervous energy, their unified command presence offering a anchor of village stability that balanced extraordinary circumstances with reassuring familiarity. Mrs. Tuggles caught her husband's eye with the briefest of meaningful glances.

Near the windows, Marjorie Blight maintained her dignified bearing despite obvious discombobulation, her careful attention to proceedings betraying someone who'd endured considerable worry about recent events. Every so often, her gaze would flicker toward the door, as though calculating distances.

Miles Penrose had positioned himself strategically near the French doors, his characteristic stoicism intact despite the extraordinary circumstances. His war-trained posture remained alert whilst his observant gaze swept methodically across the assembled company, noting each nervous gesture and furtive glance with professional assessment.

"Throughout our investigation," Cecily continued, moving to the mantelpiece where she could address everyone properly, "we encountered red herrings, misleading clues, and circumstantial evidence pointing in various directions."

She paused, ensuring complete attention before beginning systematic revelation.

"Initial assumptions focused upon port wine as the poison delivery system. However, recent revelations suggest the port itself remained uncontaminated—indicating a considerably more sophisticated methodology."

A collective intake of breath suggested everyone was following her reasoning with keen attention.

"Canon Bott," she said gently, turning toward the increasingly pale clergyman, "your fictional research provided remarkably accurate technical information about alkaloid poisoning. Dosage requirements, symptom progression, delivery methods—all enabling effective implementation by someone possessing clear intelligence on poisoning methods quite unknown to most law-abiding mortals. The final reveal in your chapter titled 'A Brimful of Secrets' was positively masterful—and dare I say, rather alarmingly thorough for a man of the cloth!"

Canon Bott's complexion had progressed from pale to positively ashen. "I never intended," he stammered, his voice barely above a whisper whilst his hands fluttered anxiously over his manuscript, "that creative writing would provide a veritable handbook for actual criminal activities!"

"Naturally not. Your research remained entirely academic —until someone with rather desperate motives recognised its practical applications for solving problems that conventional Christian forgiveness simply couldn't address."

Dr. Bell shifted in her chair with the obvious discomfort of someone discovering their professional expertise had been rather thoroughly exploited.

"Dr. Bell unwittingly provided legitimate medical consultation," Cecily continued with diplomatic delicacy, "sharing knowledge that complemented Canon Bott's literary endeavours to create what one might call a comprehensive poisoner's guide—quite a collaborative partnership."

"Purely academic information!" Dr. Bell protested, though her defensive tone suggested dawning awareness that good intentions provided rather poor protection against criminal application.

Lady Fenella, who had been following these revelations with the rapt attention of someone attending a particularly thrilling theatrical performance, chose this moment for a magnificent interjection.

"Harold warned repeatedly about collaborative guilt!" she announced with the triumphant glee of a woman who'd just solved a particularly vexing crossword puzzle whilst everyone else was still struggling with three across.

"Indeed," Cecily acknowledged with a slight smile, "the combination of clerical research and medical expertise provided the perfect combination. One might almost admire the scholarly approach—were the subject matter not quite so deadly."

She moved closer to the windows, where afternoon light illuminated her face with dramatic effect.

"The actual murder method proved remarkably elegant in sophisticated simplicity. Rather than contaminating port supplies with attendant risks for innocent parties, our criminal employed aconitine—a naturally occurring poison from the monkshood plant—mixed into an oil and administered in plain sight."

The revelation captured everyone's attention, demanding macabre admiration.

"Bellweather's book, 'The Gentleman's Deadly Secret,' provided me with the final piece of the puzzle," Cecily said, her voice carrying quiet authority. "In which a man's fashionable attire becomes the murder weapon," She paused deliberately, allowing her words to settle upon the assembled company. "The one you read only recently, Lady Fenella!"

Lady Fenella drew herself up with lofty indignation, her peacock feathers trembling with offended dignity. Her jewellery caught the afternoon light with dramatic flashes of self-righteous protest.

"I hardly see how my literary pursuits relate to murderous activities!" she declared with wounded pride, though her sharp eyes betrayed considerable curiosity about whatever revelations might emerge from such uncomfortable connections.

Cecily could not help but mention that perhaps Harold might have been rather partial to a spot of literary entertainment himself, since his otherworldly pronouncements bore striking resemblances to certain particularly dramatic portions of Canon Bott's text—right down to the theatrical phrasing about "collaborative guilt" and "ethereal justice."

Lady Fenella bristled magnificently at the implication, her peacock feathers practically vibrating with indignation. "I'll have you know that Harold's spiritual insights are entirely original!" she declared with the wounded dignity of a medium whose professional credentials had just been questioned at a particularly well-attended séance. "The fact that he happens to share literary tastes with earthly authors merely demonstrates his refined cultural sensibilities from beyond the veil!"

Canon Bott sat stunned at the revelations emanating from his most recently published work.

"Indeed, *'The Gentleman's Deadly Secret'* is a story much beloved by another Bellweather enthusiast in this very room," Cecily continued, her gaze moving deliberately across the assembled faces, noting subtle changes in expression that spoke volumes about guilty knowledge and carefully concealed anxiety.

The drawing room fell into profound silence broken only by the gentle tick of the grandfather clock and Pip's contented snuffling beneath her chair, blissfully unaware that his mistress was approaching the climactic revelation of her first murder investigation.

"Is it not, Miss Blight?" Cecily enquired with directly.

"The poison was administered, rather ingeniously, through contact with the skin rather than ingestion, ensuring specific targeting whilst avoiding general contamination. The perpetrator understood lord Oswald's vanity would be his final undoing."

The assembled attendees exchanged uneasy glances, each aware that a cunning murderer—possibly more than one —was hidden among them.

Marjorie maintained composed silence, her expression revealing neither pride nor shame.

"The motive involved years of systematic blackmail," Cecily continued, her voice growing stronger, "Lord

Oswald exploited family secrets for personal entertainment and financial advantage. Miss Lucy Thompson, the illegitimate child of a London scoundrel and Marjorie's sister, provided leverage for extracting payments whilst threatening public humiliation designed to destroy her reputation completely."

Sympathetic murmurs arose from witnesses recognising genuine desperation that might drive protective family members toward criminal extremes.

The moment had arrived for complete revelation.

"Miss Marjorie Blight," Cecily announced with measured gravity, "deliberately murdered Lord Oswald Crowthorne using alkaloid poison administered through a poisonous balm applied to the sweatband of his hat, employing technical knowledge obtained from unwitting accomplices to ensure fatal results whilst creating quite remarkable investigative misdirection. His perspiring brow and alcohol consumption merely amplified and quickened the poison's effectiveness."

Marjorie rose with dignified acceptance, her bearing suggesting relief about ending years of desperate concealment.

"Lady Ashcombe's summary reflects complete accuracy," she confirmed with calm directness, eliminating any remaining uncertainty. "I planned and implemented Lord Oswald's murder using information generously provided by people harbouring no knowledge of my intentions."

Her confession carried no hint of remorse.

"I regret deeply that circumstances endangered innocent persons or implicated honourable companions. Though I cannot regret protecting Lucy from systematic destruction designed purely for one man's entertainment and gain."

"You deliberately accessed Canon Bott's research and Dr. Bell's medical expertise for planning Lord Oswald's murder?" Cecily asked with remarkable composure despite facing someone who'd demonstrated such calculated preparation.

Marjorie's defensive righteousness suddenly crumbled, revealing the desperate mother beneath the criminal exterior.

"I accessed available resources for protecting my family from destruction," she said, her voice breaking slightly. "For protecting Lucy from exposure designed to eliminate her future prospects whilst satisfying one man's malicious appetite for power over defenceless people."

The room fell silent except for the soft ticking of the mantelpiece clock and Pip's concerned whuffling.

"Protection through murder," Dr. Bell said quietly. "Rather extreme methodology for family difficulties."

"Extreme?" Years of accumulated frustration poured out in Marjorie's response. "Tell me, Dr. Bell, what conventional remedies exist for preventing aristocratic blackmailers from destroying innocent young women through public humiliation designed purely for entertainment?"

The question hung in charged silence as everyone contemplated the genuine desperation that might drive respectable people toward criminal extremes.

"Lord Oswald was blackmailing you about Lucy's parentage?" Cecily inquired gently whilst maintaining careful pressure for encouraging complete disclosure.

"For years. Gradually increasing demands accompanied recently by explicit threats about public revelation." Marjorie's composure finally shattered completely. "He intended to announce Lucy's illegitimate status at the harvest festival—next Sunday, when half the county would witness her humiliation whilst he enjoyed demonstrating his power over helpless victims."

Her voice broke as the accumulated emotional strain finally gushed forth.

"He claimed detailed explanations would accompany the announcement—about Sarah's moral failings, our family's deceptive concealment, no shameful stone would remain unturned. Lucy would have been destroyed— unemployable, unmarriageable, socially ruined for his amusement."

Constable Fenchurch was clearly still struggling with confessions exceeding his village-level training.

"Miss Blight," he finally managed with authority undermined by uncertainty, "I require formal written documentation for subsequent legal proceedings involving appropriate higher authorities."

"Naturally, Constable. Though relevant evidence regarding years of blackmail may provide mitigating context for judicial consideration acknowledging protective rather than malicious motivation."

As official procedures commenced, Cecily found herself contemplating complex moral implications surrounding protective family violence and inadequate legal remedies for addressing aristocratic abuse.

"Miss Blight," she said quietly whilst others managed procedural requirements, "what arrangements exist for Lucy's continued welfare following your departure?"

Marjorie's expression revealed profound gratitude about practical concern extending beyond criminal justice considerations.

"Lucy possesses essential skills and admirable character enabling independent survival, though additional support would improve her prospects considerably," she replied with obvious maternal anxiety.

"Then perhaps suitable employment might be established through estate management requiring reliable domestic assistance, combined with educational opportunities ensuring proper development of obvious potential."

The generous offer struck Marjorie with emotional impact that transformed resigned confession into hopeful recognition that her sacrifice might ultimately achieve family protection despite the legitimate consequences of her actions.

"Lady Ashcombe," she whispered through tears, "such kindness exceeds anything I dared hope for Lucy's future. Though I hardly deserve charitable consideration given my methods."

"Everyone deserves compassion," Cecily replied with a gentle authority derived from her father's teachings about divine mercy extending far beyond human frailty.

Following Marjorie's official removal for questioning and the release of the other attendees, the morning room gradually returned to a state of tranquility, though the evidence of the week's unusual events remained. Pip emerged to conduct an enthusiastic investigation of scattered papers and abandoned teacups.

The grandfather clock chimed five o'clock with bronze authority. Outside, autumn light faded toward evening with melancholy beauty.

Her first criminal investigation as Lady Ashcombe had concluded successfully, establishing her reputation for competent amateur detection whilst confirming her commitment to ensure appropriate care for all persons entrusted to her responsibility.

"'He hath shewed thee, O man, what is good,'" Cecily mused, "'and what doth the Lord require of thee, but to do justly, and to love mercy, and to walk humbly with thy God.'"

The drawing room settled into peaceful silence broken only by Pip's gentle snoring and the soft whisper of autumn wind through ancient eaves, carrying with it the promise of new mysteries yet to unfold in the charming village of Little Codding.

28

LADY OF THE PARISH

The morning brought blessed normalcy to the Rose Room—no urgent messages, no dramatic arrivals, no mysterious deaths requiring immediate investigation. Cecily woke to the gentle sound of rain pattering against mullioned windows and the comforting weight of Pip arranged across the bed's foot like a small, warm guardian who'd successfully completed his first amateur detective assignment.

The sight of her terrier sleeping peacefully, his ears twitching occasionally at dreams involving rabbits or possibly escaped criminals, brought the first genuine smile she'd managed in days.

Mary arrived with tea and the cautious smile of someone whose world had returned to manageable proportions following extraordinary circumstances that had tested everyone's capacity for domestic tranquillity.

"Good morning, my lady," she said with renewed confidence, setting down the silver service whilst radiating relief about resuming normal household routines. "Mrs. Fotheringill mentioned you might prefer a quiet morning after... well, after recent complications requiring considerable management."

"A quiet morning sounds like heaven itself," Cecily agreed, accepting the delicate china cup with profound gratitude for simple pleasures that extraordinary circumstances could make one properly appreciate. The Earl Grey was perfect—not too strong, with just the right amount of milk. Such small mercies felt profound after a week of murder and mayhem.

"Though I believe we should arrange for Miss Lucy Thompson's arrival this afternoon. The poor girl will require appropriate welcome and orientation regarding her new position."

Mary's face brightened with obvious approval about charitable arrangements providing security for someone whose circumstances had proved tragically complicated despite personal innocence.

"The staff are quite looking forward to meeting her, my lady. From what we've heard around the village, she's a lovely girl who's had precious little good fortune. Cook's already planning something special for her first dinner."

The sentiment reflected household consensus about Cecily's generous response to the family crisis, confirming her growing acceptance as a mistress whose decisions commanded both respect and affection.

After completing morning preparations—and firmly discouraging Pip's attempts to redecorate her dressing gown through enthusiastic pawing—Cecily made her way to the breakfast room. Mrs. Fotheringill had arranged an elaborate display of bronze chrysanthemums whose autumn colours caught the light streaming through French doors, creating an atmosphere of restored domestic harmony.

"Good morning, Mrs. Fotheringill," Cecily said warmly, noting how the housekeeper's demeanour reflected new levels of comfortable authority. The defensive uncertainty about her mistress's capabilities had dissolved entirely, replaced by something approaching partnership.

"Good morning, my lady," Mrs. Fotheringill replied, her keys jingling softly as she moved to adjust a flower arrangement. "I've taken the liberty of preparing the blue guest room for Miss Lucy—close enough for convenient access whilst providing suitable privacy for someone adjusting to new circumstances. I thought she might appreciate the view of the rose garden."

The thoughtful arrangements demonstrated Mrs. Fotheringill's growing confidence about interpreting Cecily's preferences accurately, whilst the personal touches revealed genuine warmth beneath professional competence.

"Perfect arrangements, as always. You possess remarkable intuition about people's needs." Cecily paused, spreading marmalade on toast whilst selecting her words carefully. "I intend to visit the village this morning—addressing community concerns and demonstrating that recent tragic events needn't permanently disrupt our relationships."

Mrs. Fotheringill's approving nod confirmed the strategic wisdom of maintaining public confidence.

"Very wise, my lady. The village has been... animated with discussion. Your reputation has been quite thoroughly established, though I believe personal reassurance would cement matters admirably."

The drive to Little Codding provided opportunity for contemplating remarkable changes accomplished within one week of inheriting Ashcombe Hall. The De Dion puttered contentedly through lanes dotted with autumn hedgerows, whilst Pip maintained vigilant watch through the passenger window for any suspicious sheep requiring investigation.

She'd anticipated challenges involving household management, agricultural concerns, and social obligations requiring gradual mastery through careful observation and patient learning. Murder investigations hadn't featured amongst expected responsibilities, yet here she was—Lady Ashcombe, amateur detective, apparently successful at both.

The village green presented its usual charming tableau, though Cecily detected subtle changes suggesting community awareness that their new aristocrat possessed competence extending considerably beyond conventional accomplishments. Mrs. Brimley emerged from the post office with a warm wave rather than her usual nervous curtsey, whilst several children playing near the duck pond paused to call cheerful greetings.

"Good morning, Lady Ashcombe!" young Timothy shouted with uninhibited enthusiasm. "My mum says you're cleverer than Sherlock Holmes himself!"

This proclamation, delivered at sufficient volume to attract half the village's attention, caused Cecily to blush furiously whilst several adults chuckled with affectionate amusement.

"I hardly think that's accurate, Timothy," she replied diplomatically. "Though I appreciate your mother's confidence in my reasoning abilities."

The Gilded Goose proved an excellent initial destination.

Mr. Thorne's welcome radiated genuine pleasure rather than diplomatic courtesy.

"Lady Ashcombe! Precisely the person we've been hoping to see," he announced with hearty approval, his jovial countenance reflecting community satisfaction about recent developments. "There's been considerable discussion about your remarkable detective abilities, combined with generous arrangements for young Lucy Thompson's welfare. The consensus is that we're uncommonly fortunate in our new neighbour."

"Thank you, Mr. Thorne, though I merely applied common sense rather than sophisticated investigation skills. Father always maintained that most problems yielded to patient observation and Christian charity."

The modest explanation enhanced rather than diminished her reputation amongst practical people who valued competence over pretension.

Tom Pickering approached from his corner table with respectful appreciation.

"My lady, the tenant farmers have been meeting since dawn, discussing those estate modernisation proposals you mentioned. We're prepared to provide detailed assessments of current agricultural conditions—drainage problems, cottage repairs, field rotation possibilities. Everything requiring attention before winter sets in proper."

"Excellent, Mr. Pickering. Your expertise will prove invaluable for prioritising improvements."

The businesslike approach earned obvious approval from assembled farmers whose experience with previous estate management had emphasised aristocratic privilege rather than collaborative problem-solving.

Their departure from the pub was accompanied by genuine warmth and hearty invitations for future visits.

The penultimate morning appointment involved Canon Bott, whose psychological recovery required pastoral attention, acknowledging guilt about inadvertent assistance whilst providing reassurance about ultimate moral accountability.

She found him in St. Crispin's vestry, surrounded by carefully arranged sermon notes and looking considerably healthier than during recent traumatic circumstances. His manuscript portfolio sat nearby, though his relationship with fictional murder appeared to be under thoughtful reconsideration.

"Lady Ashcombe," he said with grateful emotion barely contained beneath clerical dignity. "I cannot adequately express my gratitude for your compassionate response to my literary... complications. Though I confess uncertainty about continuing creative writing following such grotesque practical applications."

Cecily, taking a seat, stated, "Canon Bott, moral themes in literature and fiction have a long and distinguished history. Your research methods demonstrate intellectual curiosity rather than criminal inclination."

Her reassurance provided visible comfort to someone whose confidence had been considerably shaken of late.

Canon Bott's face brightened. "You truly believe my writing might serve beneficial purposes rather than merely providing criminal methodology?"

"I believe your understanding of human desperation, combined with spiritual insight, could create stories offering hope to people facing impossible circumstances. Literature's highest calling involves illuminating divine mercy amidst human frailty."

Their conversation concluded with the promising chimes of a long and interesting friendship. Cecily had no doubt that the peculiar heir to her father's parish would become a pillar of the Little Codding community.

29

LUCY'S ARRIVAL

The afternoon return to Ashcombe Hall coincided with Lucy Thompson's arrival, creating opportunity for welcoming someone whose circumstances demanded extraordinary sensitivity and genuine Christian charity.

A modest trap had brought Lucy up the drive, her few belongings arranged beside her with touching care. She approached the main entrance with obvious nervousness about entering a grand household whose elegance exceeded anything her modest background had provided preparation for.

Her small carpet bag and carefully mended travelling dress spoke of determined effort to present a respectable appearance despite limited resources, whilst her posture conveyed a quiet courage.

Cecily greeted her personally at the front steps rather than delegating such important introductions to household staff.

"Miss Thompson," she said with gentleness, "welcome to Ashcombe Hall. This is your home now, and we're absolutely delighted to have you join our family."

The generous reception overwhelmed Lucy with emotion that had been carefully controlled during her recent family crisis. Her dark eyes filled with tears despite obvious efforts at composure.

"Lady Ashcombe," she managed through a voice thick with gratitude, "I cannot express adequate appreciation for your kindness toward someone whose family circumstances have created such... such terrible complications."

"My dear girl," Cecily replied firmly, taking Lucy's trembling hands, "Your aunt's actions demonstrated desperate maternal devotion, although her methods were rather unfortunate."

"Unfortunate indeed, ma'am. It seems that Lord Oswald's threats and demands destroyed my mother's happiness and drove Aunt Marjorie to desperate measures."

"Did you speak to your aunt? What manner of threats, specifically?"

"About my parentage. About exposing the truth regarding my father's identity and the circumstances of mother's marriage." Lucy's voice carried anger as well as sadness. "He claimed he could prove mother had been... compromised by a London gentleman before her marriage to Papa, and that I was illegitimate despite documentation showing otherwise."

"Did your Aunt suggest his claims were accurate?"

Lucy looked down, a tear running down her cheek.

"My real father was someone mother met during festivities when London gentlemen visited for hunting," she said finally, her voice barely audible. "A charming man who made promises about marriage whilst having no intention of honouring such commitments to village girls he considered temporary amusement."

"Do you know his identity?"

"Mother never revealed his name, though Lord Oswald claimed extensive knowledge. He'd been demanding money from Aunt Majorie for years to maintain silence, initially through reasonable amounts that gradually increased to impossible sums."

This confirmed the blackmail structure they'd theorised.

"Aunt Marjorie has been selling everything valuable to meet his demands, borrowing money from everyone possible, even considering selling her shop. But recently he claimed the amounts weren't sufficient anymore, and that he intended to expose everything publicly at the harvest festival next week."

The timing explained urgency motivating immediate action rather than continued negotiations.

"Did your aunt discuss specific plans for preventing such exposure?"

Lucy's expression suggested she knew nothing of her Aunt's desperate bid to protect her reputation.

Mrs. Fotheringill appeared with her customary efficiency, though her expression carried genuine warmth rather than professional obligation.

"Miss Lucy," she said warmly, "your room has been prepared with everything necessary for comfortable settlement. Fresh linens, adequate coal for the fireplace, and writing materials should you wish to correspond with... with your aunt during her current difficulties."

The tactful reference to Marjorie's incarceration demonstrated Mrs. Fotheringill's growing competence at managing sensitive situations involving household charity.

"Additionally," the housekeeper continued with obvious satisfaction, "we've arranged a gradual introduction to household duties enabling skill development whilst pursuing the educational opportunities Lady Ashcombe considers essential for your continued advancement. Nothing overwhelming initially—perhaps assistance with correspondence and light secretarial duties suited to your obvious intelligence."

The arrangements exceeded Lucy's most optimistic expectations.

Pip's enthusiastic investigation of their new household member provided a spirited and slobber-filled reception. His immediate acceptance, demonstrated through lively tail wagging and vigorous licking, suggested canine approval of Lucy's character and suitability for estate community membership.

"Oh!" Lucy exclaimed with delighted surprise, kneeling to receive Pip's energetic greeting. "What a handsome fellow! And so very... friendly!"

"Pip has appointed himself household greeter," Cecily explained with amusement as her terrier launched an encyclopedic investigation of Lucy's travelling bag. "Though I should warn you that he possesses strong opinions about personal belongings and considers everything his own personal possession."

"He's perfectly charming," Lucy assured her, rescuing her belongings whilst scratching behind Pip's ears. "I've always loved dogs, though circumstances never permitted keeping proper pets."

The easy interaction between Lucy and Pip provided encouraging evidence about her adaptability to household life.

As afternoon progressed into evening, Cecily found opportunity for private reflection in the library, where she and Elsie settled before a cheerful fire with the comfortable familiarity of long time friends.

Pip arranged himself across the hearth rug with obvious satisfaction about completed household security duties, whilst autumn rain created gentle percussion against diamond-paned windows.

"Well," Elsie observed, "you've certainly established your reputation as Lady Ashcombe with remarkable efficiency. One week from inheritance to solving a sophisticated murder whilst implementing charitable estate management that would impress King George himself."

"I hardly feel like I've solved anything," Cecily replied with honest humility about recent accomplishments, settling deeper into the Earl's favourite chair.

"Absolute nonsense!" Elsie declared with characteristic directness. "I heard Mrs. Tuggles describing you as 'exactly what Little Codding needed' whilst Captain Tuggles proclaimed you 'officer material.'"

"Most importantly," Elsie continued with growing emotion, "you've proven yourself worthy of the Earl's extraordinary trust in your character and capabilities. His faith has been vindicated through practical demonstration of wisdom, courage, and compassion that honour both his memory and your father's teachings."

"You know," Cecily mused, watching flames dance in the grate whilst contemplating the extraordinary week just concluded, "Father always preached that divine providence operates through ordinary people willing to serve others despite personal limitations. I never imagined such service might involve amateur detection and criminal investigation."

"Perhaps the Lord knew you'd require diverse skills for managing estate responsibilities," Elsie chuckled with gentle humour. "After all, somebody capable of nursing wounded soldiers through artillery bombardment probably possesses adequate preparation for handling village murder investigations."

A soft knock interrupted their reflection as Lucy appeared in the doorway, hesitant about intruding upon private conversation.

"I'm terribly sorry to disturb you," she said quietly, "but I wanted to thank you both properly before retiring. Mrs. Fotheringill has been extraordinarily kind with arrangements, and I... well, I've never experienced such generous hospitality."

"Lucy, dear," Cecily said warmly, gesturing toward the remaining chair, "please join us. You're family now, and family doesn't require formal permission for conversation."

The invitation brought fresh tears to Lucy's eyes as she accepted the offered seat with obvious gratitude.

"I keep expecting to wake up and discover this is all a wonderful dream," she admitted softly. "Amidst the worry of Aunt Marjorie's situation and the discovery of Lord Oswald's threats... to find myself here, treated with such kindness despite our family's criminal complications..."

"I cannot condone your Aunt's actions," Cecily added gently, "but every family harbours secrets requiring compassionate understanding rather than harsh judgment."

The reassurance provided Lucy with emotional relief about family loyalty, whilst encouraging optimism her future prospects despite tragic complications.

"Your aunt acted from love, however misguided her methods," Cecily continued. "And everyone speaks so well of your character. We shall ensure she receives proper legal representation."

Lucy's shoulders relaxed slightly at this promise. "You truly believe there's hope for her?"

"I believe," Elsie interjected with gentle firmness, "that Lady Ashcombe has proven herself remarkably resourceful at finding solutions where others see only problems."

The three women sat in comfortable silence, watching the fire settle into glowing embers.

"You know," Lucy said finally, her voice stronger now, "Aunt Marjorie always spoke of providence working through unexpected channels. She'd be amazed to see how her desperate act led me to such extraordinary kindness."

"Perhaps," Cecily mused, "that's precisely how providence intended it. Your aunt's love for you, however desperately expressed, has brought you home to Ashcombe Hall."

As if sensing the significance of the moment, Pip opened one drowsy eye, surveyed his expanded pack with obvious satisfaction, and returned to his dreams with a contented sigh.

"Welcome home, Lucy," Cecily said softly, and meant it with all her heart.

The young woman smiled through her tears—the first truly peaceful expression she'd worn since arriving. Outside, the rain continued its gentle benediction over Ashcombe Hall, where three women and one devoted terrier had found themselves exactly where they belonged.

The Earl, Cecily thought with quiet certainty, would have approved entirely.

30

A LETTER IN BLACK INK

The third week of November had settled over Ashcombe Hall like a familiar embrace, bringing the sort of peaceful domesticity that Cecily had scarcely dared hope for during her tumultuous first days as mistress. Morning light streamed through the estate office windows, illuminating ledgers spread across the mahogany desk in neat arrangements that spoke of gradually mastered responsibilities.

Cecily paused in her correspondence, stretching fingers that had grown accustomed to managing tenant reports rather than preparing Sunday school lessons. The transformation still surprised her—from vicar's daughter wrestling with the coal bill to Lady Ashcombe overseeing drainage improvements and cottage repairs across hundreds of acres.

"The Pickering fields are responding beautifully to the new drainage," she murmured, making careful notes in her increasingly confident hand. "And if the weather holds, we'll have the last cottage roofs completed before December."

Such mundane concerns brought profound satisfaction. Estate management involved complex challenges, certainly, but nothing approaching the moral complications of tracking poisoners through dinner parties.

Pip had appointed himself chief administrative supervisor, positioning beneath the desk where he could monitor all activities whilst maintaining access to any dropped correspondence requiring canine investigation. His warm weight against her feet provided welcome companionship during long hours of learning responsibilities her vicarage upbringing had never encompassed.

A gentle tap at the door interrupted her concentration. Mrs. Fotheringill appeared, bearing the morning post, though Cecily detected something approaching fondness in the housekeeper's manner these days.

"Letters from London regarding the drainage contracts, my lady," Mrs. Fotheringill announced, setting down the silver salver. "And what appears to be an invitation from Lady Pemberton for Christmas festivities."

"Christmas already?" Cecily laughed, accepting the elegant invitation. "How optimistic of Lady Pemberton, considering our recent excitement involving mysterious deaths and amateur detection work."

"I believe your reputation has spread considerably beyond Little Codding," Mrs. Fotheringill replied with unmistakable pride. "The county appears quite taken with their clever new neighbour who solves murders."

She was examining a particularly encouraging report from the agricultural college when Lucy appeared in the doorway, hesitating with obvious reluctance to interrupt administrative duties.

"Lady Ashcombe," she said softly, "I've completed the library inventory you requested. Though I discovered several rather... curious historical documents that might warrant your attention."

Lucy's confidence had flourished remarkably during recent weeks. Her intelligence and gentle nature had won universal staff affection, particularly from Mrs. Fotheringill, who valued her assistance with complex household accounts.

"Excellent work, Lucy. What sort of curious materials?"

"References to previous mysterious incidents involving unexplained deaths," Lucy explained. "Documents spanning decades, suggesting Ashcombe may harbour considerably more secrets than recent events indicated."

Before Cecily could respond, rapid footsteps announced Elsie's characteristic approach.

"Cecily!" she called from the corridor, voice carrying unmistakable urgency. "Rather odd young fellow at the front door, claiming special delivery for Lady Ashcombe specifically."

The emphasis on personal delivery suggested circumstances exceeding routine correspondence.

Cecily gathered her shawl with growing curiosity whilst Pip's ears pricked forward with professional awareness that unusual visitors often provided developments worth thorough investigation.

The scene at Ashcombe's imposing entrance proved remarkably mysterious for such a peaceful morning. A thin boy of perhaps twelve stood fidgeting nervously, clutching an envelope bearing an elaborate seal. His clothing suggested neither village origins nor gentry connections—simply practical garments providing few clues about his background.

"You're Lady Ashcombe?" he asked with a broad accent suggesting origins well beyond Oxfordshire.

"I am. You have something for me?"

"Yes'm. Special delivery requiring personal attention. Very particular instructions about proper delivery only to her ladyship specifically."

He extended the envelope with obvious relief. The thick paper bore expensive quality, whilst an elaborate black wax seal indicated either formal importance or dramatic affectation.

"Who provided these instructions?" Cecily inquired, accepting the envelope with growing unease.

"Can't rightly say, m'lady. Gentleman didn't provide particulars, just specific directions about delivery and immediate departure afterwards."

The boy's eagerness for swift retreat suggested he was less than comfortable with his assignment. After appropriate compensation, he hastened down the drive with obvious relief.

The envelope felt thin—a brief, mysterious correspondence. Black wax obscured any identifying impressions, making origins impossible to determine through casual examination.

Despite sensible reservations about potentially dangerous contents, curiosity overwhelmed prudence. Cecily carefully broke the seal. The distinctive wax cracked with finality, releasing whatever secrets dramatic concealment had preserved.

A single sheet of expensive paper bearing elegant handwriting conveyed formal education despite its ominous message. Three lines of careful script suggested deliberate economy for maximum impact:

Lady Ashcombe,

You solved one. But how many more sleep in Ashcombe's soil?

The past never rests as quietly as the living might prefer.

No signature, no identifying marks, no explanation— simply stark words carrying unmistakable implications about mysteries requiring future investigation, despite her determination to focus upon peaceful estate management.

Her first detective adventure had concluded successfully through divine assistance. Future investigations might prove more challenging, yet her father's training in faithful service provided a foundation for trusting that appropriate wisdom would always be supplied.

"Secrets may slumber in Ashcombe's soil, but they will not rest forever," Cecily said, tucking the letter back into the envelope. "There is nothing covered that will not be revealed, nor hidden that will not be known."

Whatever secrets awaited discovery, Lady Ashcombe would prove equal to every one of them.

Her inheritance was secure, her reputation established, her calling confirmed.

And somewhere in Ashcombe's ancient soil, secrets slumbered—waiting for Lady Ashcombe's particular talents to bring them, at last, into the light.

～

THANK YOU FOR CHOOSING A PUREREAD BOOK!

We hope you enjoyed the story, and as a way to thank you for choosing PureRead we'd like to send you this free Special Edition Cozy, and other fun reader rewards…

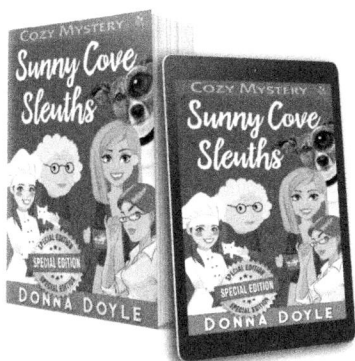

Click Here to download your free Cozy Mystery
PureRead.com/cozy

Thanks again for reading.

See you soon!

OUR GIFT TO YOU

AS A WAY TO SAY THANK YOU WE WOULD
LOVE TO SEND YOU THIS SPECIAL EDITION
COZY MYSTERY FREE OF CHARGE.

Our Reader List is 100% FREE

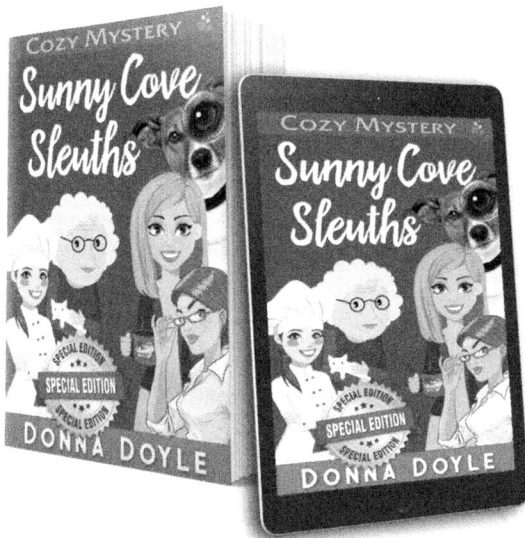

Click Here to download your free Cozy Mystery
PureRead.com/cozy

At PureRead we publish books you can trust. Great tales without smut or swearing, but with all of the mystery and romance you expect from a great story.

Be the first to know when we release new books, take part in our fun competitions, and get surprise free books in your inbox by signing up to our Reader list.

As a thank you you'll receive this exclusive Special Edition Cozy available only to our subscribers...

Click Here to download your free Cozy Mystery
PureRead.com/cozy

Thanks again for reading.
See you soon!

Printed in Dunstable, United Kingdom

67918163R10150